Scoring OFF THE FIELD

A WAGS NOVEL

A WAGS NOVEL

NAIMA SIMONE

This book is a work of fiction. Names, characters, places, and incidents are the product of the author's imagination or are used fictitiously. Any resemblance to actual events, locales, or persons, living or dead, is coincidental.

Copyright © 2018 by Naima Simone. All rights reserved, including the right to reproduce, distribute, or transmit in any form or by any means. For information regarding subsidiary rights, please contact the Publisher.

Entangled Publishing, LLC
2614 South Timberline Road
Suite 105, PMB 159
Fort Collins, CO 80525
Visit our website at www.entangledpublishing.com.

Brazen is an imprint of Entangled Publishing, LLC. For more information on our titles, visit www.brazenbooks.com.

Edited by Tracy Montoya
Cover design by Cover Couture
Cover art from Shutterstock

Manufactured in the United States of America

First Edition March 2018

To Gary. 143.

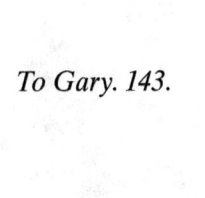

Chapter One

"I quit." Tennyson Clark mentally slapped a palm to her forehead, hating that her nerves made her mumble, so the announcement sounded much more like, *"Mwy scmhit."*

When one was declaring one's independence, one definitely shouldn't sound like a squirrel with a mouth full of nuts. She sighed. So much for being firm and assertive.

Fortunately—or unfortunately—her best friend of fifteen years, Dominic Anderson, was fluent in Tenny Speak. And since his attention snapped from the phone in his hand to focus completely on her, treating her to the full blast of his bright blue stare, she assumed he'd interpreted her garbled statement correctly.

"You quit?" he repeated, confirming her assumption in a calm and even tone. She wasn't in the least bit fooled. Ten years ago, he'd used that same voice when he'd threatened to cut off Calvin Shephard's dick if the bully dared touch her again.

Often, having someone in your life who loved, protected, and knew you better than anyone else on the planet was a comfort and gift. Then other times, it sucked hairy ape balls.

This was one of those times.

"Yes, that's what I said," she stated, fighting not to fidget under the power of his beautiful, scalpel-sharp gaze.

Damn, it was so unfair. After looking into those eyes for fourteen of her twenty-five years, she should've been immune to their beauty and intensity. But as Foster Mom #2 had been fond of saying, "A fair is a shitfest of carnies and rides. It ain't got fuck-all to do with life." Quite the poet, Foster Mom #2 had been. But in her own way, she'd been right on point.

Life had handed Tennyson a great deal—a mentally unstable mom, a parade of foster homes and parents who'd ranged from apathetic to scary, a plethora of schools, zero stability. But one thing it had never offered her was fairness.

For instance, this pathetic, secret, cringe-worthy unrequited love for her best friend and employer.

Well...*former* employer, as of five seconds ago.

Dom slowly straightened from his lazy sprawl on the couch and set his cell down on the coffee table in front of him with an ominous *thunk*, causing her hope that he would take the news well to crumble like a Taylor Swift relationship past the ninety-day mark.

Suddenly, he wasn't Dom, her childhood friend, but Dominic Anderson, celebrated All-Star, four-time Pro-Bowl quarterback for the Washington Warriors. As the leader of one of the best teams in the NFL, he commanded a legion of behemoths on a daily basis.

"Look," she muttered, "I'm trying not to be pusillanimous about this, and you glaring at me isn't helping."

Dom blinked, his only reaction. "From the context of your sentence, I'm guessing that means you're trying not to be a pussy about dropping this atom bomb that you're abandoning me as my PA."

This time, she couldn't prevent flinching. "I would've gone with cowardly or faint-hearted, but very good," she complimented, trying to insert a little levity into the conversation. #Epicfail.

Without waiting for his reply—which was sure to contain at least one F-bomb and probably a couple of goddamns—she launched up from the huge armchair that swallowed her Lilliputian frame whole but was perfect for the giant across from her. She shot from the suddenly too-stifling confines of his man-cave den and dashed for the kitchen as if a naked Jason Momoa waited for her next to the pots and pans rack.

Like everything else in his Mediterranean-style home in the wealthy Seattle suburb of Kirkland, Dom's kitchen was mammoth. It was also total culinary porn. Weak light from the late morning October sun trickled in through the large windows, brushing the marble counters and the island in pale, watery streams. Walnut cabinets with glass fronts lined two walls above high-end appliances that would have Mario Batali whining in jealousy. A huge window that stretched from the ceiling to above the sink granted gorgeous views of Mount Rainier, the beautiful evergreens that surrounded the house and property, and an endless stretch of sky. At least on sunny days. Today, that sky was overcast, and the rain that the Pacific Northwest was known for pinged against the glass, but it was still beautiful. So rich and vivid.

Still, the masterpiece of the kitchen, and what she loved most, was the beautiful stainless-steel stove with its six eyes; large, self-cleaning oven; and multiple settings. Yes, if she could have sex with it, she probably would. Considering the last couple of times she'd been with a man, the stove would no doubt generate more heat.

The best thing about the room, though, was that Dom—also known as Chef Boyar-Don't—couldn't boil an egg without shells and yolk ending up splattered on the ceiling.

When he'd had the kitchen designed, it'd been for her, because she loved to cook. The precision and creativity of preparing food soothed her, grounded her.

She didn't need a psychologist to explain why. Control. At first, it'd been her mother who'd supplied her meals…and often added extra ingredients guaranteed to make Tennyson sick, warranting another trip to the hospital emergency room. Later, in the foster homes, she'd had no choice but to eat whatever she'd been given, some of it indigestible. Or if it'd been adequate, there hadn't been enough of it. When she'd grown older and was able to provide for herself, food had been one of the first things she'd exerted autonomy over. What she ate. The quality of it. The quantity.

In this moment, even as she declared her independence in another area of her life, she still turned to the thing that comforted her.

Striding to the enormous refrigerator, she opened it and scanned the contents, finally settling on French toast, bacon, and an omelet. Scooping up the needed ingredients, she kicked the door closed and deposited the food on the island.

"You can't dodge this conversation by going all Iron Chef," Dom growled.

She hadn't heard him enter the room; for a six-foot-five, two-hundred-and-twenty-five-pound giant, he was remarkably light on his feet. But she hadn't needed to catch his footsteps to know he stood behind her. She *felt* him. Like her body transformed into a tuning fork specifically adjusted to perceive him. Her skin sensitized, her belly tightened, her heart beat at a slightly elevated pace. Over the years, she'd had to work hard to hide her reaction from his all-too-perceptive gaze. She'd become a master at deception. At pretending she loved Dom like an annoying and overprotective big brother when her feelings were anything but platonic.

The decade-long charade was…exhausting. But the

alternative—admitting to him that she wanted to be one of those tall, gorgeous, sexy supermodels, actresses, or even random football groupies he fucked like sex was the last loaf of bread on a grocery store shelf during a snowstorm—scared the hell out of her. No, sir. Quite some time ago, she'd been on the receiving end of his gentle, soft, and utterly humiliating rejection. And not to mention the pity. The awful, mortifying pity. No thanks. Never again. The scar from the first time they'd had that Friend Zone talk hadn't fully healed even after all these years. Damn if she would tear open another wound.

"I'm not dodging anything," she said, removing the chopping board from one of the island's side drawers. "I'm fixing breakfast while we discuss."

"Yeah, let's discuss." He leaned on the marble top, his rock-hard abs brushing her elbow and arm. *Shit*. She fumbled the onion but quickly recovered, cursing that glancing touch that now had electric currents zinging up and down her spine. Images of the corrugated ladder of muscles that covered his stomach bombarded her mind. If she didn't know better, she would agree with those snide comments on Instagram that snarked about the images of Dom being Photoshopped to show a corded, ripped eight-pack. But she knew better. Dom had never possessed a single modest bone in his body, so she'd been treated to unhindered views of his bare torso many times through the years.

Masochism, thy name is Tennyson Clark.

Forcing the panty-melting picture from her head, she focused. "It's not like I'm leaving you tomorrow. I'm giving you a month's notice, and I'll stay to train my replacement."

"The hell, Tenny?" he snapped, frustration ripe in every sharply enunciated word. "I don't want a replacement. And I damn sure don't want a month's notice."

"Well, you have one, and you're going to get the other."

She shook her head. "Dom, it's past time I left—"

"Really?" he interrupted. "Says who?"

"Says me," she ground out. "You know, *me*. The person in charge of my life and what happens in it? That me."

He blew out a hard breath, pushing off the island. She glanced up in time to catch him thrusting his fingers through his dark brown hair. Over the years, he'd worn it ruthlessly short, like a Roman centurion, or so long the strands had brushed his shoulders. Lately, the loose waves grazed his carved-from-stone jaw, making him resemble the guy who played Jamie Fraser in *Outlander* more than he usually did.

The thick, soft-looking hair should've seemed incongruous with the chiseled lines of his face. And they might have if not for the black, dense fringe of lashes that accentuated the cobalt depths of his eyes and that sensual, almost lush mouth that made a woman imagine all the dirty things he could do with it. And undoubtedly do well. His face was a stunning work of art.

God, his face. It'd sold everything from electric razors to luxury cars. And it haunted her every night, starring in her most secret, erotic dreams.

Glancing away, she desperately reined in the thoughts before they seeped into her expression, and he glimpsed the taboo longing that was as much a part of her as the wild curls on her head and the birthmark under her left ear.

He didn't want that from her. Not her longing. Not her desire. Definitely not her heart. He'd made that abundantly clear years ago when she'd made the godawful mistake of getting drunk one night and letting slip how she felt about him. Oh yes. Abundantly clear.

"I know this is surprising—" she began again.

"No, Tenny. Finding out Santa Claus wasn't real, *that* was surprising. *La La Land* discovering they hadn't won Best Picture was surprising. Kanye having a mental breakdown was surprising…"

"Was it? Was it really?" she interjected. But at his narrowed glare, she sighed and pantomimed zipping her lips shut. But seriously, Kanye losing his shit hadn't been that shocking.

"You up and quitting out of the blue is a straight kick in the nuts I didn't see coming. And in the beginning of the season? I should be enjoying my day off before focusing on winning against the Steelers, but instead, you hit me with this."

"Well, I'm sorry, but when would've been a good time? Besides," she added, anger beginning to lick at her chest, "this isn't about you."

"You're right. It's about *us*." He waved a hand back and forth between them. "We're a team. We always have been."

A team. The words pierced her like a poison-tipped arrow straight to the heart. So innocuous, so…kind. And that kindness killed her. Because it underscored how he would always see her—a kid sister, a pal. It emphasized her utter foolishness in continuing to carry this torch for him. It reminded her that one day she would watch him settle down with one of the women who flocked around him, while she remained alone and emotionally bruised.

Inhaling, she tried to explain again. "I get this is anathema to you…"

"Small words, Tenny. Small words," he snapped.

"Fine," she retorted, her temper crackling like oil hitting a hot pan. "I know this fucks with your day, but it's done. And you're not changing my mind."

Marching to one of the cabinets, she yanked it open and removed a big mixing bowl. Dom grabbed the other side of the bowl and pulled on it, but she jerked it back. For the next few moments, they engaged in a truly childish tug-of-war.

"For godsakes," she muttered, releasing the bowl with a

scowl.

Before she could grab another, he smacked the dish on the counter and, palming her waist, hiked her in the air and plopped her on the marble in front of him.

She gasped as he flattened his hands on either side of her hips and leaned forward, caging her between his big body and the large window behind her. She tried to edge back so every shallow breath didn't include his scent of soap and freshly washed skin, and the deeper, familiar fragrance of cedar and heavy, sultry rain. How many times had he come to visit her in one of her foster homes after he'd been adopted, the fragrance of cedar clinging to his shirt and hair from the Dayton lumberyard where he'd worked part-time?

Even now, she had to curl her fingers around the edge of the counter to keep herself from burying her nose in the crook between his shoulder and neck—the space that she'd claimed as her own at eleven years old—and just breathe him in. As a child, that place and his scent had been a comfort. They'd meant safety. Now, both still brought comfort, but they also wreaked havoc on her senses, on her pulse. Caused a decidedly sinuous, *unfriendly* heat to wind its way through her veins and culminate in an achy, throbbing beat between her thighs.

The struggle was real.

"Now, no more evading. Talk," he ordered.

Rebellion sparked within her at the imperious tone and the expectation to fall in line, but she deliberately inhaled, calming herself as well as the resentment that flickered inside her like a struck match. A foolish resentment because he couldn't know how much his nearness affected her; since the first time she'd stupidly and recklessly admitted her love for him, she'd made a concentrated effort to ensure he'd never know, and that her misplaced desire wouldn't jeopardize their friendship. Still, he wasn't a dumb man—far from it. He knew how much she cared for him, even if only in a sisterly way. Using his hotness and her unflagging loyalty against her was sneaky.

Anger and his close proximity formed a dangerous combination, and if she wasn't careful, she'd allow both to weaken her resolve and reveal information she wanted to keep close to her chest.

"I don't know how much clearer I can make it, Dom," she said. "I've been your personal assistant for five years now. Five years. It started out as a job you made up as a way you could give me money without it seeming like charity—"

"I did not," he objected. But when she lifted her eyebrows, he grumbled, "If you weren't so goddamn stubborn, I wouldn't have needed to do it. Still, that was then," he added. "Now, I can't imagine how I ever functioned without you."

"And that's the problem," she stated, a vise tightening around her heart at his words. "We have to find out how to function without each other." Especially her. Because her life—her heart—could no longer revolve around him. Not when the feeling wasn't reciprocated.

"That's bullshit," he rumbled. "Why? We're a—"

"Team, I know," she finished, barely managing not to roll her eyes. "And we don't need to work together to continue to be a team. Dom, I have a bachelor's and master's in social work, and I'm doing nothing with them."

"So that's it? You have another job?"

"No," she hedged. Technically, she wasn't lying. She'd applied for several jobs in the field in which she'd earned her degrees. And one was even a strong maybe. But nothing had come through as of this morning.

"Then what's the rush? Is it something I did?" He studied her, searching her face as if he could find the answer there. Again, she fought not to duck her head to avoid the penetrating scrutiny. "Was it when I snapped at you last week about that meeting with Under Armour? 'Cause you know I didn't mean to hurt your feelings. I was tired and upset about the loss to Denver. If I need to apologize again, then I'm sorry."

She snorted, rolling her eyes. "Please. You seem to have a convenient forgettery." At his narrowed gaze, she huffed out a breath. "A convenient faulty memory. The Under Armour meeting was the third time you'd popped off at me that day. But if I stayed mad every time you got snippy, I'd have smothered you in your sleep years ago."

"You're either lying or nervous. Probably both," he announced. "You've used three of your vocab words in twenty minutes. That's a definite giveaway. So you want to try this again?"

Had she said that having someone in your life who knew you better than anyone else sometimes sucked hairy ape balls? Correction. It sucked hairy King Kong balls.

Most people surmised her learning new vocabulary words was a hobby. No one but Dom understood the real reason and its origin.

After hours and hours in doctors' offices and hospitals where the only reading materials were medical magazines, she'd made figuring out the unrecognizable words a game. While her mother had weaved lies upon lies about her daughter's health, and the doctors falsely diagnosed Tenny with ailment after ailment based on manufactured symptoms, she'd discovered what bibasilar, gastrointestinal, and abdominous meant.

By the time Dayton, Ohio's Child Protective Services removed Tenny from her mother's "care," she may have emerged with an irrational fear of hospitals, but she'd also come away with a stellar vocabulary for a ten-year-old.

Learning new words had become a habit, a coping mechanism. And when she was stressed or nervous, she tended to spit them out more than usual. As he'd so *graciously* pointed out.

"I need to get a life outside of organizing yours," she stated. "Find my own way. Stand on my own."

He stared at her for several long moments. Blinked. "I have no idea what the hell that means. You been watching Dr. Phil again?"

"Asshole." She shoved him out of the way and jumped down, stomping across the kitchen—and away from the knives.

"What?" Dom crossed his arms over his chest. "You're going to tell me that doesn't sound like the life-affirming bullshit he spouts. Maybe I should add a Texas accent to it." He cleared his throat, and then in an exaggerated southern twang, drawled, "We teach people how to treat us."

"I take it back." She scowled. "You're not an asshole. You're an ass-a-hole."

His crack of laughter bounced off the walls of his pristine kitchen. "Is that a new vocab word?"

"Yes," she shot back over her shoulder, marching past the gleaming pots and pans hanging from the iron rack. *You can't bash him over the head with a frying pan*, she reminded herself. At least not until he saw reason. Then she might swing for the fences. "It's a noun. Definition. When someone is so much of an asshole, they need another syllable."

She didn't acknowledge his "Okay, that was a good one," as she stormed out of the kitchen. This is what she got for trying to do the right thing. She should've just went with her first inclination and found a replacement on her own. Then one day, have the new person just show up. That way she could've avoided this whole asinine conver—

Elegant, long fingers wrapped around her bicep and halted her halfway across one of the two dining rooms in his huge home. Strong, muscled arms banded around her waist, holding her in a gentle but implacable embrace. Helplessly, she ogled the taut skin, tanned to a burnished gold from hours of football practice under a summer sun. Even the thick vein running along his forearm had her clamping her lips shut before she submitted to the desire to run her tongue along it. Bite it.

Her heart thumped against her rib cage, and she cursed the involuntary reaction to his touch. *We're pissed at him*, she reminded the traitorous organ. But all the damn ticker did in return was pound harder when his embrace tightened and pulled her against an equally hard body.

"Don't go," Dom murmured in her ear. "I'm sorry for being an ass-a-hole."

Since he couldn't see her face, she risked closing her eyes and letting her lips part on a silent gasp. She concentrated on preventing a shudder from rippling through her, betraying how good his tall frame felt pressed to her smaller one. At her five-feet-five height, he towered over her, surrounded her in a wall of flesh, muscle, and warm skin. Made her feel safe even as his nearness presented a danger to her composure, her carefully constructed pretense of friendship...her sanity.

Her stomach clenched, knots twisting and tightening until she wanted to cry "Uncle." She should have been well acquainted with the unrelenting lust that transformed her into a human pretzel. And on one level, she was, but on the other... How could this sweet, taunting torture ever become old hat? Not when it seemed to increase, deepen, and grow hotter with each year that passed.

Not when his every embrace and touch screamed of sibling love, and she wanted those soft brushes of his knuckle across her cheek, those tender kisses to her forehead, those strong hugs to brand her with passion. A passion he seemed to reserve for other taller, slimmer, more sophisticated, *less sisterly* women. Not for shorter, curvier—okay, pudgier—

socially awkward, sibling-like women...in other words, her.

No, for her, he would never feel that kind of desire.

Memories flooded her.

Drunk dialing him after her first fraternity party. Him picking her up from the frat house and driving her to his home. Her, confessing to him how she'd been approached by one of the guys there, but she didn't want any of them... She just wanted him. That she'd been in love with him for so long and none of those "boys" could compare. The terrible morning after when he'd prepared breakfast, then sat her down and explained how they could never be more than friends. How their relationship was too important, too valuable to damage it with sex. The horrible, humiliating pity in his eyes as she'd tried to brush off her admission as shit-faced ramblings.

God, she'd never forget that pity.

At the time, her younger self had placed the blame on Tara, the cold-hearted bitch who'd damn near destroyed him—and his fledgling football career—the year before. But now, with distance, she could accept that Dom just didn't see—or want—her as more than a friend. The truth hurt like hell, but there it was.

Over the years, she'd managed to lock away those feelings—well, maybe shut the door on them. And for periods of time, she'd been successful, going out on the occasional date, hanging out with friends, managing to convince herself that she'd moved on. That she no longer carried a torch like an Olympic relay runner. But then, inevitably, there would come occasions like these. When Dom would affectionately cuddle or touch her. When his innocent, friendly behavior cracked open that door again, just enough for her feelings to flood back in.

It was a painful, embarrassing cycle.

And after bumping into his latest one-night stand as she did the walk of shame out of his house, she'd decided it was time to end it, once and for all. Inhaling, she extricated herself from his arms even as her body yelled, *WTF?* Making sure her we're-just-buddies mask was firmly in place, she pivoted to face him, arms crossed over her chest. As if the gesture could protect her heart from any more of his unintended and completely oblivious damage.

"Look at it from my point of view, Tenny," he said, spreading his hands, palms up. "All this time, I thought you were happy working with me. You've never said otherwise. Never even hinted you were discontented. And now, out of the blue, you're telling me I suck as an employer and you're out. How the hell do you expect me to react?"

"I never said you suck," she grumbled, guilt worming its way through her. Which was ridiculous. Somehow she doubted, *"Hey, I'm quitting because I need to get a life instead of standing around and having my heart torn out of my chest every time you bang a girl like a snare drum"* would go down very well. "And how do I expect you to react? I don't know, disappointed, yes. But also happy for me. Everything isn't about you, Dom."

"Now you're just making me sound like a self-absorbed shithead." He gripped the back of his neck, and the muscles in his arm flexed as he squeezed the strong column.

The hem of his T-shirt rose, gifting her with a glimpse of the broken pocket watch tattoo on his lower stomach, the wicked sharp cut of his hip bones, and that tantalizing V that she'd followed with her tongue during many late-night fantasies... Swallowing a groan, she mentally slapped a palm to her forehead. *Focus, damn it.*

Clearing her throat, she glanced away from him, lifting a shoulder in a half shrug. "If the stink fits..."

Chuckling, he closed the small distance between them, and grasping her shoulders, pulled her close and pressed a kiss to her forehead. She briefly closed her eyes, savoring the touch of his lips to her skin. Even the light caress had her thighs pressing together and a longing for *more* tumbling through her like a furious riptide. So easily he dragged her under his scent, his power...*him*.

Even if she'd experienced a moment of indecision about her choice to leave, this overwhelming yearning for everything he couldn't—wouldn't—give her cemented her reasons.

"I am happy for you." She snorted and felt his lips curve in a smile. "Okay, I'm trying to be. I never claimed I wasn't a selfish bastard. If anyone knows that, you do."

Not selfish, just a tad bit controlling. Fine, a *ton* controlling. But like he understood her quirks for vocabulary and cooking, she got where his need originated. Even though his path through Dayton's foster care system had ended with adoption while hers had not, they'd both emerged from the same system with scars.

"Just..." He tunneled his fingers through his hair, shoving the thick strands out of his face. "My contract is up at the end of the season. You know how it is, always competing for your spot. I've been doing fine, but I also need to fucking kill it this season to get re-signed."

She scoffed, offended on his behalf that the front office would even *consider* replacing him. He was a damn god on the field. "They wouldn't get rid of you."

His pinched her chin. "If only you owned the team," he teased. "All of my focus has to be on football, Tenny. I can't worry about what's going on behind the scenes, and if you're not there having my back, I will. I get you want to leave..." He frowned. "Okay, I don't get that. But can you at least stay through the season?"

She stared at him, resolve wavering. Dom had been her rock for the past fourteen years. He wasn't asking for much considering all that he'd given her—protection, security, a college education, a job...hope. And in the grand scheme of things, what were six more months? She could hold off...

No. She knew herself, knew her weakness. And it was Dom. The longer she stayed, the more excuses she would find to remain as his PA, in an apartment ten minutes away from him. Eventually, she would convince herself this half life she'd been living wasn't so bad. That she didn't need love or independence or a family of her own. For the first time since she'd walked into that foster home and laid eyes on him standing in the doorway of a tiny living room, she was strong enough, determined enough—hell, desperate enough—to walk away from him.

And in her soul, she understood that if she didn't do it now, she never would.

"You'll be fine," she assured him, stepping back and breaking his hold on her. She should've built up an immunity to his touch through the years, but no such luck. Louis Pasteur couldn't invent an inoculation for Dominic Anderson. "And I'll make sure my replacement has Teflon skin, knows all your likes, dislikes, and annoying habits. I won't leave you hanging."

"Tenny," he began, but she cut him off with a hard shake of her head that was as much for him as it was a reminder to herself.

"Dom, this *is* happening. I won't be working for you at the end of the month."

After a long moment, he nodded. "All right then."

The placid reply had suspicion crawling through her. Tilting her head, she narrowed her gaze on him. And a whole lot of *oh shit* sprinted through her at his composed expression...and the determined glint in his eyes.

She sighed.

This hadn't gone as well as she'd hoped.

At. All.

Chapter Two

Dom strode off the practice field, removing his helmet. Behind him, the defense still continued to run the new plays Coach Declan and their defensive coordinator had outlined in their team meeting that morning. In just four days, they would meet the Steelers and their explosive offense at home on CenturyLink Field. If the Warriors had a chance of winning, the defense had to be on their game. So did the offense, for that matter. They had to be better than good, better than prepared. They had to be on their shit.

So did he.

Squinting, Dom could just see the special teams running their drills on the second of the practice fields of the Norman B. Rice Athletic Center. The complex, located in Redmond, lay about twenty minutes outside of Seattle. Though they and Washington's other professional football team both played at CenturyLink Field, the Warriors practiced at the athletic center built for them about five years ago. Smaller than the Seahawks' Virginia Mason Athletic Center, the property boasted an indoor facility, administrative space for the team's front office, two outdoor fields, a training area, several meeting rooms, and a full-service and staffed cafeteria. And it was Dom's home away from home.

Swiping a hand over his damp hair and face, he grabbed one of the water bottles on the sideline and dropped to one of the benches. After several gulps, he planted his elbows on his knees and surveyed the drills on the field. He didn't glance to the side when a large body settled beside him. Zephirin Black, one of the greatest tight ends in the league and Dom's other best friend, studied the plays beside him in silence.

"The defensive line isn't on their stance quick enough. They're not coming off the ball at the snap," Dom observed.

"No," Zeph agreed. "And the linebackers are reacting to the pass first instead of to the run. They'll get it together, though. Coach Yancie will get them right." After several moments, he said in that quiet, calm way of his, "I heard Tenny quit as your PA."

Dom scowled. "How the hell did you—wait, let me guess. Ronin."

Zeph shrugged.

Ronin Palamo was also their friend—and the biggest gossip on the team. The man should write a damn blog, for godsakes.

"So it's true?" his friend pressed, tipping his own water bottle to his mouth for a deep gulp.

"Yeah." Still frowning, he stared off into the distance, no longer seeing the players on the field. "She said she needs her own life. Whatever the fuck that means."

Like yesterday, when Tenny had dropped her announcement, a bruising band tightened around his chest—the same tension that invaded him when he stood on the sidelines during a game, watching it go to hell and unable to do anything about it. The tension that squeezed the breath from his lungs when his adoptive mother had been diagnosed with breast cancer, and he could do nothing to help her as she endured debilitating chemotherapy treatments.

A loss of control. Utter helplessness. The bitter flavor of failure.

He'd had too much of the first two in his life and vowed not to condone the third.

Unwillingly, he glanced across the field and watched Colton Jensen, the twenty-four-year-old backup quarterback for the Warriors, throw the football back and forth while the quarterback coach looked on. The guy had a great arm. Not as good as Dom's...yet. A lot could happen in a season—a bad run of games, an injury, subpar performances. On any given Sunday, Colton could be the new starting quarterback, and it could be Dom watching from the sidelines. And with his current contract ending at the end of the season, the Powers That Be might decide to take a chance on a younger player with potential to be great rather than stick with a quarterback who was sliding toward thirty, an expiration date for some football players.

The thought—the pressure—had been keeping him up at night lately. He had to eat, drink, breathe and sleep football to prove he was worthy enough.

He couldn't afford to have any distractions.

Which was why he needed Tennyson in his corner, having his back.

She'd said, "I need my own life." He'd heard, "I'm leaving you." The thought had been—how had she put it?—*anathema* to him. And not just because he would be losing an excellent personal assistant.

Yes, she made his life run better than his Aston Martin DB11. But more than his PA, she was his friend. His *best* friend. The person who knew him longest and better than anyone, even Zeph and Ronin. And they'd seen each other's dicks.

Though his brain demanded he stopped acting like a pussy, the primitive, instinctive part of him roared in denial and anger. Because that part knew he was losing her, no matter how Tenny worded her resignation.

"I'm guessing it means exactly what she said," Zeph said, continuing the discussion Dom wanted no part of. "Tenny has two degrees. It's kind of unrealistic to believe she would use them to arrange your life, buy gifts for your girlfriends, and order your groceries for the rest of her life."

"One, I don't have girlfriends, and two, I've never asked her to do any of that."

"What about when she bought that diamond bracelet for the actress? The one in that superhero flick?" Zeph countered.

"It was a present to thank her for the last-minute tickets to the premiere of her film," Dom argued.

The other man stared at him for several seconds. "You fucked her, though."

"Shut up," Dom grumbled.

Snorting, Zeph shook his head. "You have to let her go, bruh."

"Let who go where?" Ronin plopped down on the other side of Zeph, his dark hair scraped back into one of those man buns. Although, he had to admit, his friend pulled it off where most men just looked pretentious and damn dumb. Might be because Ronin wore it for expedience and not fashion. Dom silently snickered. Not that the wide receiver was known for his style—unless you called ripped jeans, washed-out T-shirts, and scuffed-up boots fashion. On the football field, Ronin was a beast. But off? The man was the very definition of laid-back.

"Tennyson and off on her own," Zeph supplied.

"Oh, right," Ronin said. "I completely agree. Like my sisters are ever fond of telling me, 'It's hard to get dick with

The Hulk breathing down their necks.'" He scowled. "They might have a point. Because the thought of any motherfucker putting his dirty hands on any of my sisters does make me want to go *smash*."

"Jesus." Zeph shook his head, loosing a loud crack of laughter.

"Tenny isn't leaving because of a guy."

His friends didn't utter a word, but the look they exchanged might've as well blinked *Yeah, okay*, over their heads in neon green.

"What the hell is that supposed to mean?" he snapped, an inexplicable and admittedly disproportionate irritation scraping the underside of his skin like brand-new sandpaper. "If she had a man in her life, I would be the first to know about it."

She wasn't like him. He didn't do relationships—he fucked. Relationships were time-consuming, and football was his wife, mistress, and side chick. He'd learned the hard way that he couldn't serve two masters.

Tenny, on the other hand, wasn't the kind of woman satisfied with casual flings. She wasn't built like that.

"That's what we're saying," Ronin said. "Tenny's life revolves around you, your job, your meetings, your errands, your needs. What about hers? She's a beautiful, smart, sexy-as-hell twenty-five-year-old woman. With a social life that totals to zilch, bagatelle."

"Bagatelle?" Dom repeated, not even attempting to keep the *WTF* out of his tone.

"You like?" Ronin's grin flashed from the middle of his thick, lumberjack beard. "I learned it from Tenny. But allow me to prove my point." Leaning back, he yelled, "Erikson!" and waved another player over.

The tall, lean fullback's dreads brushed his shoulders as he strolled over. "What's up?"

"Tennyson, Dom's PA." Ronin waved a hand toward Dom. "You remember her?"

"The hottie with the hair and bangin' body? Hell yeah. Who could forget all that—" Erikson curved his hands, cupping them, but when he met Dom's glare, he dropped his arms and grinned. "Hair. Who could forget all that hair?"

Ronin arched an eyebrow at Dom. "See? One I'll-hand-your-boys-to-you-in-a-gunny-sack look, and Erikson's cupping himself and running in the opposite direction."

"I wouldn't say running," the other man interjected with a frown as he backpedaled toward the practice field. "Walking briskly, but never running unless it's after a ball."

"This is bullshit," Dom snapped, the discomfort and annoyance swelling in his chest, along with an anger that simmered just beneath like a seething cauldron at both Ronin and Erikson's description of Tenny.

Hottie? Bangin' body? An image of Tenny infiltrated his mind as if conjured. Of unruly, dark, almost black curls that brushed slender shoulders and framed a delicate face dominated by big, chocolate brown eyes, interesting angles, and a wide, surprisingly carnal mouth. So petite, her halo of spirals just brushed the underside of his jaw; she was a little thing. But she was a road map of curves and dips. Full breasts that many women paid good money to get surgically. A tiny waist that made the flare of hips even more pronounced. Proportionally long legs that belonged on a runway model, not a pixie like her. And the smoothest, loveliest shade of brown that reminded him of the natural pine he handled at the lumberyard he worked at as a teen.

She resembled one of those fifties pinups with her hourglass figure and full curves. But sexy as hell? She was pretty, yes, but still...Tennyson.

His best friend. His constant in a life that had more twists and turns than a post corner route. Even when he'd hit rock bottom in college, she'd been there. Even when their relationship had been a little strained, he'd still never doubted her loyalty. Even after she'd had a beer-goggles moment and declared her love for him, they'd weathered that short-lived storm, and she'd still had his back. She was the only family he had left to depend on.

"Face it, bruh," Zeph said, interrupting his thoughts with a slap on the shoulder. "You're cock-blocking and don't even realize it."

"Actually, I think it would be called pussy-blocking since she's a woman," Ronin argued.

"Don't make me punch you in the face," Dom warned Ronin. "And I call bullshit, again. Tenny would have no problem telling me to fuck off if I got out of line."

"Would she?" Zeph stood, stretching his long arms above his head. "You get away with murder when it comes to her. She puts you ahead of herself all the time."

"If that's true, then why is she so gung-ho to leave me?" God, now he sounded like a sulking child. What next? Probably a full on man-trum if Tenny didn't change her mind about quitting.

"Look, D," Ronin said as their coach blew the whistle, signaling their break was over. He chucked his bottle into a nearby garbage can with a flamboyant jump shot, then turned to Dom with a shrug. "She's getting a life, which, by the way, I don't think is a bad thing at all. It was bound to happen. Now you just have to pop that titty out of your mouth and deal."

"For once, I have to agree with the lumberjack." With another slap on the back, Zeph slipped his helmet on his head and followed Ronin back to the field.

Frowning, Dom lightly jogged after them, but his mind remained on their conversation. Even as he ran the new plays for Sunday's game, he couldn't shake free of it.

They were wrong. Yeah, maybe he was a little

overprotective when it came to Tennyson, but he didn't prevent her from having a life outside of her job. He didn't scare off the men she dated. *When* she dated, that is.

Okay, so there was the time in college when she'd had sex for the first time with some asshole frat boy.

She'd been this innocent, and a little naive, freshman, and the guy had been a junior majoring in art history of all fucking things. Nothing about that big-as-a-tank motherfucker with his faux hawk, tatts, and tight T-shirts had said "art history." Red flag number one. Dom's first time meeting the guy, and Dom's douche-dar had started pinging like a metal detector. He knew the type: spoiled frat boys who zeroed in on the incoming freshmen so they could tally how much ass they got like the women were punches on a scorecard.

Yeah, Dom had paid him a visit and might have mentioned something about him peeing through a straw for the rest of his life if he hurt Tenny. The asshole had broken things off with her the day after their talk, and she'd been hurt, but better sooner than later after the schmuck dragged her name, reputation, and heart through the dirt. He'd been down that ugly, pitted road, and he'd do anything to protect her from that kind of pain and disillusionment.

If that made him a cock-blocker—or pussy-blocker, as the case may be—then screw it. She was *his* to protect. Had been from the moment her social worker had ushered her into the Shermans' house, and he'd looked into her too-carefully-composed-for-an-eleven-year-old face. That detached expression had been a punch to the gut. But when he'd met her gaze... Every emotion absent from her features had been swirling like a wild storm in those pretty brown eyes. In that instant, all the anger, bitterness, and grief that had been firmly entrenched in him since his parents' deaths in a car accident two years earlier had eased. Because at fourteen, he'd found his purpose. Taking care of this too-quiet, scared little girl.

That resolution hadn't changed in the fourteen years that followed. It'd been why he'd remained at Ohio State after his junior year instead of entering the draft a year earlier, waiting until Tennyson finished high school. And when he'd signed with the Warriors the same year she'd become a legal adult and had been emancipated from the foster care system, he'd brought her to Washington with him. He'd provided her with a place to live and had even paid the tuition her scholarships hadn't covered with his salary.

Football and Tennyson—they were his motivations for everything in his life since that fateful day they met.

And the thought of losing her, of not being there to protect her from a world he'd tried his best to shelter her from, had his gut twisting in so many knots, it probably resembled bondage rope play gone wild. Because he didn't need a magic eight ball to predict how this would play out. First, she quit. Then she suddenly would become busy—too busy for him. Their daily interactions would become every day, then weekly, then even less than that. Eventually, their presence in each other's life would fade as she found new friends…replacing him.

The irony didn't escape him.

During his sophomore year of college, he'd fallen in love with another student, Tara Jacobs. She'd been beautiful, sophisticated, fun, great in bed. He'd been so wrapped up in her, he'd done the same things he feared would happen with Tenny: he spent less time with her; he placed Tara as a priority above Tenny and football; his relationship with his best friend suffered, as did his game. In fact, his focus had been so divided, he'd missed several practices for her, endangering his scholarship and his place on the team—which would have made it difficult if not impossible to catch a pro coach's eye after graduation.

He'd lost control over the most important things in his

life. Only to discover that the woman he'd adored only loved being the star quarterback's girlfriend. She liked being in the stands and having the camera pan to her more than she liked actually being with him. He'd overheard the words from her lips at a party one night while she'd gossiped with a friend. *"He's hot and can fuck like a horse, but he's not the brightest bulb in the box. Not to mention a total hick. But they're saying he could be a number-one draft pick, so I can put up with him."*

He'd dropped her ass, fixed things with Tenny, and refocused on his game. After that, nothing else mattered but getting drafted so he could provide the life he and Tenny never had.

To an outsider, he might look like he was on the verge of losing control again, with his contract up for renewal. But he wasn't about to let it happen. No shortcuts. No distractions.

Forty-five minutes later, when he and the team headed to the locker room for a media session, his resolve had returned. Solidified. Somehow he had to convince Tennyson that they belonged together. He needed her. They needed each other. They were family.

This was one game he intended to win.

Chapter Three

"Now this guy has tons of experience. One of his former employers was even a football player. He's definitely in the Give a Call pile," Tennyson said, scrolling through the résumés submitted by an applicant for Dom's new personal assistant. "What do you think?"

When she didn't receive an answer, she glanced up from her laptop. Across from her, Dom sat sprawled on his home office's couch, his gaze fixed on the mounted TV. He aimed the remote toward the wide, flat screen, carelessly flicking through the channels.

"Hellooo," she called. When that didn't garner a reaction, she picked up a pen and tossed it across the room, the blue cap hitting him square in the forehead. He'd practiced throwing the football around with her when they were kids so much that she had a killer arm.

"Damn it, Tenny," he growled, picking the ink-filled missile up off his lap and flinging it onto the sofa cushion next to him. "I just got back from practice. Can I relax for five minutes?"

"Please." She rolled her eyes. It was Monday, his lightest day of the week aside from Tuesdays, his day off. "It's the first practice after a game. You had meetings and walk-throughs all day. Suck it up."

"Don't forget the media interviews where I had to explain why I threw an interception in the red zone and missed open receivers on crucial downs. Oh and let's not forget those two sacks," he muttered. "Apparently, 'because I fucked up' isn't a socially acceptable excuse."

She winced, catching the disappointment and frustration under the sarcastic reply. No one was harder on Dom than Dom. He'd become one of the best quarterbacks in the league because of his perfectionist attitude. But he'd always been that way. Whether it was staying out on the high school football field practicing his throws and snaps with the coach long after the rest of the team had called it quits, or studying for hours until he could quote a classroom textbook, or leading his college team to a NCAA National Championship.

Dom hated failure. And even though the Warriors had defeated Pittsburgh the week before, he would still consider the loss to Atlanta the day before a failure.

Sometimes—no, often—she worried about his unrelenting pursuit of perfection and control. She got it; no one got it more than her. He'd had the perfect life—a home, middle-class parents who provided for him and loved their only son, and security. Then, at the age of eleven, he'd lost the two people who'd cherished him most and had been thrown into a system that wasn't exactly warm and affectionate to most children. But to a boy who'd known nothing but adoration and unconditional love, it'd been hell. For three years, his life had been strange and chaotic. By the time he'd been adopted by his high school coach at fifteen, no more of the carefree boy he'd once been existed. That iron will had been forged in the fires of grief and loss. But that same iron will had been her security for the last fourteen years of her life.

And then there'd been the clusterfuck that was Tara.

Tara. From Georgia. Tenny silently snorted. How very original and *Gone with the Wind*-ish. Yeah, all these years later, and she still wanted to pile drive the scheming bitch.

Most people would crumble under the weight of the responsibility and pressure of being the face and leader of a professional football team, of being under the unrelenting scrutiny of the media and public, of being at the constant pull and demand of the Warriors organization and companies whose products he endorsed. Of providing the emotional and financial support to a foster sister.

Then again, "most people" weren't Dom. He relished leadership roles—excelled at them. The more he managed, organized, and commanded, the happier he was. Though he would never admit it, the more secure he was.

But she was tired of being one of those responsibilities.

Of being a burden.

Dom would never see her as a desirable woman, but he could at least view her as an equal.

Which meant she had to force him to make a move to hire her replacement. It'd been two weeks since their initial discussion about her leaving, and he'd found every excuse to avoid talking about it. From practice, to meetings, to getting a new tattoo, to watching a freaking *Homicide Hunter* marathon on TV, the man had become an expert in the art of ducking and dodging. But not tonight.

"Losing sucks, and it won't be the last time, so drag that big-boy cup on, and move on. Besides, these applicants aren't going to hire themselves."

"You're damn right I need a *big*-boy cup," he grumbled, reluctantly shifting aside as she sank down to the couch with the laptop.

Unbidden, her attention dropped to his thighs, and she

bit back a groan. The gray sweatpants did nothing to conceal the considerable bulge of his cock. A thick, melting heat slid between her thighs, settling there with a low throb. He wasn't even erect—not with her sitting beside him—and the length rested against his damn thigh. Part of her wondered why she even carried a torch for him. If by some chance pigs sprouted wings and unicorn horns, and he looked at her with lust instead of brotherly affection, she'd probably faint in maidenly horror at her first sight of his dick.

"Did you just check out my package?" he drawled.

Oh shit on a stick. Fire blazed up her chest and neck, and she battled not to let a blush lay siege to her cheeks. Shrugging, she met his amused gaze and feigned a nonchalance that didn't exist. "Don't worry," she said, patting his forearm. "I didn't see a thing. Maybe if I had my magnifying glass…"

"Smart-ass." He bumped her shoulder with his, and the *friendliness* of it sent both love and pain shooting through her. Grabbing the computer, he set it on his lap with a sigh. "Fine. Let's get this over with."

Elbowing past the emotional shoving match inside her, she scrolled down the résumé on the screen. "I think he's a great candidate. He has six years' experience and, like I said, two of them with another player. That's—"

"I don't like him," he interrupted, closing out the document with a tap to the mouse pad.

"What?" She gaped first at the screen that now showed her inbox instead of the résumé, then at him. "What the hell? Why not?"

"Because he's obviously a job-hopper. Three jobs? Can't commit. Something must be wrong with him," he replied calmly. "Probably snoops through his employers' homes when he's alone and sells shit to tabloids."

"How in the world do you get that from a *résumé*?" she demanded. Although, he might have a point. Three same-level jobs in six years didn't look that great, now that she thought about it. "Fine," she muttered, clicking on the next email. "Here's one that seems like a good fit. She's worked as a PA for the last four years, and it's been only *one* employer," she added, sliding him a glance. "She's worked for a corporate executive and just scanning over everything that fell under her list of responsibilities, she's more than capable of handling this job."

"No."

She blinked at the flat refusal. "Why not? You barely even glanced at it."

"She attached a picture with her résumé." He pointed at the headshot of a pretty young woman in her mid-twenties with shoulder-length blonde hair and green eyes. "No one does that unless they think their looks will help them get a job. I don't feel like getting ass thrown at me along with my mail. Next."

"Are you freaking kidding me?" She glared at him. "Your ego is almost as big as the *self-reported* size of your dick."

His blue gaze didn't waver. "Next."

With more force than necessary, she clicked the mouse to close the document and pulled open the next. But that candidate suffered the same fate as her predecessors. As did the following three. Used a fancy font, too flighty. Fresh out of college, didn't have enough experience. Left an employer after ten years, probably fired and couldn't be trusted. And on it went.

By the time she closed the last résumé, she wondered if "acting like an ass" was just cause for murdering someone. Any jury who'd suffered the asinine excuses and stubborn refusals she'd just endured couldn't possibly convict.

"What else you got?" he asked, as if he wouldn't torpedo any future applicant. Well, if she'd had any more applicants for him to torpedo. Damn.

"Dom one, Tennyson zero." She jabbed a finger at him. "This isn't over."

A corner of his mouth quirked. "It isn't my fault you didn't bring me qualified candidates," he said, taking the laptop from her and pulling up a new browser window.

"Bullshit," she snapped. "I organize your calendar, answer your emails, arrange your travel, and run your errands. It's not rocket science, and I'm damn sure not the only person who can do it."

"Then why haven't you found anyone competent enough to— *What the hell is this?*" He leaned closer to the computer, a scowl replacing the smug smile.

She glanced at the screen. And immediately closed her eyes. Fuck a duck, where was a mudslide, earthquake, or the Rapture when you needed them? Whether the floor cracked open or Jesus Christ came back, she wasn't picky. Just as long as she could suddenly disappear.

Seconds later, she lifted her lids, and nope. Still sitting on the couch, and the page for the dating site she'd signed up for three weeks earlier was still there, too. *Damn.* Note to self: next time, log out, not just minimize.

"Tennyson," he growled, and she shifted her attention from the smiling profile picture of Adam Rutheridge, the guy she'd been communicating with for the past several days, to Dom.

"What?" she asked, opting to go with innocence. Not that she had to explain her decision to give online dating a try. This whole thing fell under the heading of "Not Dom's Business." She reached for the laptop, but he nudged her hands away. Heaving a heavy, much aggrieved sigh, she shook her head. "You act like millions of people don't frequent dating sites every day."

"You're not millions of people," he pointed out, voice tight and low. "And what do you need this," he waved a hand at the screen, "for?"

"Well, unlike you, I don't have the opposite sex throwing themselves at me in droves," she pointed out.

"That's bullshit," he countered. "You're beautiful. Any man would want to date you."

Except him. To him she was beautiful like the little sister who would be pretty even with braces, pigtails, and bad acne. The platitude was nice but empty. "Right," she scoffed. "Which is why all the women you take home are short, have ass for days, and carry about twenty more pounds than they should." When he scowled, parting his lips to object, she waved him off. "I don't know why you're so upset. It's not like this is a new thing."

"These sites are filled with nuts and perverts who like to make lampshades out of women's skin."

She blinked, her lips falling open. "Um, wow. You might want to cut back on *Homicide Hunter*."

"This isn't a joke." He jabbed a finger at Adam's cute blue bowtie dotted with miniature gold poodles. "His user ID is HappilyEverAdam for fuck's sake," he snarled.

She lifted a shoulder in a half shrug. "I thought it was clever and sweet." When his growl rolled through the room like a foreboding clap of thunder, she held her hands out, palms up. "Give me some credit. It's not like I'm going to meet him at midnight in an abandoned warehouse. I know the rules. Public place which I'm driving to and from. He can't exactly skin me alive in a crowded restaurant, can he?" she drawled.

But her sarcasm bounced against him like a medicine ball...filled with lead.

An anger that had been directed at her one time in her life—when she'd given her virginity to that asshole frat boy Craig Wesley—darkened his eyes to a broody indigo.

"Tell me you don't actually plan on meeting this guy," he

said, his voice even, calm. Ominous.

"Not that it's any of your business, but yes."

"Forget it. Not happening," he ordered in the same tone he used to snap out plays on the football field. Hard. Quick. With a full expectation of being obeyed.

Oh hell no. A matching fury surged within her, hot, swift, and with thorns.

"As much as you like to believe you're my brother, you're not. I don't need to ask your permission to date or consult you on *how* to go about it. When you start letting me veto or approve your hit-it-and-quit-its, then we can talk. But until then? Back. Off," she snapped.

Those storm-filled eyes narrowed on her, his full lips flattening into a grim line. Silence, thick and alive with tension, thrummed between them. Intensity seemed to emanate from his powerful body, and he studied her with that same penetrating, concentrated focus. The weight of it touched her face with a pressure that was almost tactile. As if his gaze had transformed into a hand that gripped her face between large, calloused fingers, holding her in a firm, implacable grasp.

Anger had fueled the quick rise and fall of her chest. But something darker, rawer, more carnal slowly replaced it. Lust pumped in and out of her lungs, stroking the underside of her skin in an undulating caress, beading her nipples into tight, aching points. Pooling between her legs and teasing the pulsing flesh there.

His gaze dropped to her breasts, and the air in her throat sizzled and evaporated. The black, V-neck top she wore seemed too skimpy and too stifling at once. She couldn't force a word past her suddenly too-tight esophagus as he frowned and returned his scrutiny to her face.

Too afraid of herself, of her body's reaction to him, to remain seated on the couch, she launched to her feet. The heels of her ankle boots clicked against the hardwood floors as she crossed the room toward the desk—and safety.

"So, anyway," she said, clearing her throat and gathering up her purse and laptop bag. Damn, he still had the laptop. Screw it, she'd get it later. No way in hell was she going back over there to him while her body buzzed like a live wire. "I'll start looking for more—"

"What are you wearing?"

She glanced up, met the frown that still marred his brow, then peered down at herself. What? The neckline of the top dipped lower than those she usually wore. But coupled with the skinny jeans and boots, she looked pretty damn good.

"What's the problem?" She held her arms out. "It's a shirt and jeans."

His inspection roamed over her, and it was nonsense, but she could feel the sweep of it from her hair that she'd pulled into a top knot, down her torso and legs, and back up. Her skin might as well as have been bared to the visual touch from the way it tingled. She bit her bottom lip, trapping the moan flirting at the back of her throat inside.

His hooded stare lowered to her mouth, and the flock of birds in her stomach scattered like buck shot had just exploded over their heads. Frozen, she stood there as that blue gaze slowly lifted and met hers. The same tension that had driven her from the couch darkened his eyes, and for a moment, whispers of excitement and unease curled through her.

But then, he blinked. And whatever she'd thought she'd glimpsed—more likely imagined—had disappeared. She exhaled.

"Are you going somewhere? Maybe meeting Mr. HappilyEverAdam tonight?" he pressed, standing.

Quickly, she resumed packing away her mouse and day calendar. It didn't require all the extra attention and focus she gave it, but anything was better than ogling her best friend's body as he crossed the room toward her. Or being caught ogling her best friend's body…by said best friend.

"Nope," she said, belatedly answering his question.

"When is that supposed to happen?" he asked, handing her the laptop, the casual innocence in his voice not fooling her. At all.

"None of your business," she replied in the same breezy tone.

"Tennyson," he cajoled, but she shook her head.

"Forget it." Finished packing up, she grabbed her bags and gave him a blinding smile that might have contained just a hint of desperation. She needed to get out of his presence as soon as possible before her frayed nerves caused her to do something stupid. Like throw herself at him and beg him to fuck her. "Gotta go, or I'm going to be late."

"Go where?" he insisted, following her out of the office and into the hallway that led to the front of the house.

"Bye." She didn't glance over her shoulder or wave as she jerked the door open and exited as if the hounds of hell nipped at her heels and she was wearing steak stilettoes.

Only once she pulled out of his wide driveway did she finally relax, exhaling a huge breath of relief.

For a moment there, when she'd imagined the flicker of heat in his eyes, she'd almost believed that maybe, just maybe, he might feel… She shook her head. He'd killed that fantasy a long time ago. Yet, here she was, actually hoping she'd glimpsed desire for her in his gaze. Only the Good Year blimp with "He's Just Not That Into You" emblazoned on the side would've been a bigger clue that she needed to get away from him as soon as possible. Entertaining the idea that Dom wanted her would be disastrous. She had to find her replacement.

Immediately.

Chapter Four

"Yum," Tennyson hummed, smacking her lips at the lime with a hint of orange flavor chilling her tongue. She swiped a fingertip through the salted rim of the glass. "What's this called again?"

Renee Smith grinned. "A frozen Top Shelf Margarita with Patron Silver tequila. Only the best for you, my friend," she announced. "I mean, what better way to celebrate your new phase in life than with Margarita Monday at Doyle's?"

The bar in Pioneer Square was a favorite hangout for them as well as the other members of their small group—Dom, Ronin, Zephirin, and another friend of theirs, Jason Wilder. Though three of the guys were famous and easily recognized professional football players, they weren't harassed when they came to the tavern. They were sometimes approached for autographs, but for the most part, the regulars were so used to them, their presence didn't create much of a stir—a reason they all enjoyed hanging there and didn't mind traveling the half hour—for Dom and Tennyson, at least—to the bar.

Currently, just Tennyson, Renee, and Sophia Cruz,

Zephirin's girlfriend and the newest member of their circle, occupied one of the back booths for a girls' night out.

"What is that supposed to be?" Sophia pointed to Renee's drink. The glass contained the same light green liquid as Tennyson's, but an upturned Corona bottle sat in it like a huge cocktail umbrella.

"It's a CoronaRita." She beamed, taking a healthy sip before offering the glass to the gorgeous app developer. "Want to try it?"

"Uh, no." Sophia shook her head, the blue tips of her dark hair catching the low lighting of the room. "I'm the DD, remember?" she muttered, picking up her beer bottle, obviously still disgruntled about her designated driver status.

"Right. That damn short straw." Tennyson snickered and extended her arm across the table to Renee. "Gimmee. I'll take her sip."

"Hell no," Renee objected, pulling the glass toward her chest and holding it in a protective gesture. The bottom of the bottle bumped her nose. "You're a lightweight. This will stick your dick in the dirt fast."

Sophia sputtered, quickly snatching up a napkin and dabbing at her mouth and chin. "Stick your dick in the dirt?" She howled with laughter. "Is that a euphemism for getting wasted?"

Renee grinned, nodding. "I learned it from that guy from Alabama I was seeing. He was boring as hell, but he had the cutest phrases. And a big dick that bent to the left. That I'll miss even more than his southern colloquialisms." She sighed, removing the Corona.

While Sophia sputtered into her beer, Tennyson snickered, admiration sliding through her. And not just because Sophia, owner of her own app-development company, and Renee, a public relations consultant for the Warriors franchise, were successful professionals. Both of them wore confidence like the latest New York Fashion Week creation and were independent and strong. Everything Tennyson strived to be one day.

Hopefully, "one day" would arrive sooner rather than later.

"Okay, a toast." Sophia held up her beer, Tennyson and Renee quickly following her lead. "To Tenny. May you kick ass in your new start and career. Well, not literally since, y'know, you'll be working with kids. But then again, maybe, if you come across some really horrible parents…" She scowled, as if envisioning these horrible parents.

"Alrighty then," Renee drawled, clinking her glass to Tenny's and Sophia's. "As Pollyanna was saying," she snickered, "we're thrilled for you, girlfriend. And it's about time!"

Tennyson sipped her margarita, both the alcohol and her adoration for the two women leaving a warm glow behind. "Thank you, guys. At least you're happy for me. Can't say the same for Dom." She snorted. "Let's just say he wasn't very receptive to the idea of me leaving."

"You've been his PA for years," Renee objected, her drink sloshing close to the salt-encrusted rim as she set it hard on the table. "Your life can't revolve around him forever."

"I pointed that out," Tennyson added. "And his reply? We're a 'team,'" she said, scrunching her fingers in air quotes.

"True, he probably had a What the Hell moment, but I bet part of it was concern, too. And because he's a man, just didn't know how to voice it." Sophia tilted her head. "Aren't you a little worried, too? You have to be a little scared stepping out there on your own after so long. God knows, I was."

Tennyson intended to walk away from the only safety net she'd ever known. Hell yes, she was worried. And terrified. Especially considering a new job might mean moving hundreds of miles away from Seattle, her friends, and Dom.

To Dayton, Ohio.

The decision to apply for a position with Dayton's Offices of Families and Children hadn't been made on a whim. Considering her history, majoring in social work had been a no-brainer for her. And the opportunity to work in and try to bring change to the very system she'd been a part of? The idea that she could potentially protect and help kids like her had inspired her to apply.

Still, she'd spent months battling insecurity, fear, doubt, and an avalanche of "what ifs" over it. What if she couldn't make it on her own without his strength and influence? What if the loneliness of not having the one constant in her life sabotaged her determination to start over? What if Dom suddenly realized he was madly in love with her? What if she failed to find that special someone for her because she judged every man against her best friend?

She silently snorted. The first two questions she had no answers for, but the last two?

Not a chance in hell, and if the past was anything to go by, a distinct possibility.

But while she couldn't change Dom's eternal come-over-here-so-I-can-give-you-a-noogie, big-brother feelings toward her, she could do something about deeming every man Quasimodo when compared to Dom.

Distance. It was her last hope to get over this futile love for him and to save their friendship. Because, eventually, that love would devolve into resentment. Envy already scored her every time she arrived at his house to greet the latest one-night stand performing the walk of shame out the front door. Or when she caught sight of him pushed up against another woman, his mouth covering hers, his hands skimming her body. When those same women freely touched him with flirtatious strokes to his chest and arms or whispered in his ear, knowing their attention wouldn't be rejected but welcomed.

No, before she let that envy twist into jealous anger and ruin their relationship, she would leave first.

"Of course I'm nervous," she finally replied to Sophia's question. "But I can't let fear keep me from having a life. Dom doesn't understand that."

"Why don't you just tell Dom you love him?" Sophia asked.

The soft question doused Tennyson in icy shock, breaking over her in a frigid wave. How did Sophia…? Tennyson had never confessed her deepest secret to anyone. God only knew because He was, well…God.

"You're risible." Tennyson laughed, the sound high and shaky even to her ears. She tried to play it off, dismissing her friend's words with a flick of her fingers.

"I'm not trying to be funny," Sophia countered with a flash of a smile. "That's the definition, right? You've used that word before."

"Wait, what?" Renee stiffened, slowly lowering her glass to the table. "Love Dom? What's she talking about?"

Her lips forming a small "o," Sophia glanced from Renee then to Tennyson. "Um, she didn't know? I thought…" She fell against the back of the booth, lifting her bottle to her mouth. "I'm just going to…" And took a deep swallow.

Renee's laser-sharp focus remained on Tennyson. "You're in love with Dom? And why am I the last one to know?"

Tennyson spread her hands wide over the table, her palms up. "I didn't—"

"She didn't tell me," Sophia jumped in, shooting Tennyson an apologetic glance. "I thought you knew. I mean, one look at the two of them together, and I guessed. It was obvious to me…" She trailed off, wincing. "Sorry, Tenny."

Fire blazed up her neck and streamed into her face. If

she could sink under the table and find a crack in the floor to crawl into, she'd live as a troll right there in the bar's back booth.

One look at the two of them together, and I guessed. It was obvious to me...

Sophia's words pinged against Tennyson's pride like rocks striking a windshield, leaving webbed cracks and fractures behind. Who else knew? Did Dom? *Oh fuck...* Panic and horror competed for dominance in her chest.

"Dom doesn't know," Sophia gently murmured, reading Tennyson's mind. Sophia covered Tenny's balled fist with her hand, squeezing lightly. "Zephirin would've mentioned it."

The assurance alleviated only a little of the mortification still setting her face ablaze. Zeph knew. Did that mean Ronin...? She immediately dismissed the thought. If Ronin did, that meant everyone did. The man's mouth flapped harder than a loose shutter in a Kansas tornado.

"I wish someone would've mentioned it to me," Renee interjected. "Why didn't you, Tenny?" Her friend couldn't hide the accusation or hurt in her voice, and both had Tennyson reaching across the table for Renee's hand.

"Because who wants to admit something like that to themselves much less anyone else? For ten years, I've been lusting after my best friend, and all he sees is the little sister he never had. It's pathetic. And humiliating. Can't forget humiliating."

"My question still stands. Why don't you just tell him the truth?" Sophia lifted an arm and signaled their waitress who stood at a nearby table. With a circular motion over their heads, she gestured for another round of drinks. "I mean, at this point, what do you have to lose?"

Tennyson laughed, and the sound grated against her throat. "Uh, the little pride I have left? Years ago, Dom had the Friend Zone conversation with me and laid it out there that he would never feel more than friendship toward me. Did I mention this was after I foolishly confessed to him how much I loved and wanted him?"

"Damn." Sophia winced. "Ouch."

"Yep. Ouch. Though I tried to play it off, it hurt our relationship for a little afterwards. I'm not going to risk that again. Besides, have you looked at me lately?" Tennyson leaned back and swept a hand up and down her torso. "Between the time I arrived and now, did I somehow grow eight inches, lose fifteen pounds, and get rid of my ass? Dom goes for women like you," she said, flicking fingers at both of her friends. "Not me. And even if he did somehow crack his head, forget that I'm his precious BFF, and we had sex, how long do you think it would be before he lost interest? Then his guilt would only fuck up the relationship we have. No thanks. I don't need to be anyone's regret."

"That's not true," Sophia objected, but Renee remained silent. Because her other friend had experienced exactly what Tennyson described.

Renee and Jason Wilder, the last member of their tight circle, had grown up together along with Ronin in the Seattle area. Earlier in the year, Renee and Jason had decided to add sex to their relationship. And that had been the demise of the friendship they'd had since childhood—and the easy closeness of their group. Now, the two of them could barely stand to be in the same room with each other, and the rest of them were like family caught up in the aftermath of divorcees. It hadn't come down to choosing sides yet, but if the bitterness between the two didn't ease up, the rest of them might eventually find themselves in that awkward position. Sophia hadn't met Zeph yet when all this went down, but the disastrous fallout had made the others vow to remain in the friend zone with each other. None of them wanted another clusterfuck like Renee and Jason's to tear the rest of the group apart.

"Is that why you're quitting as his PA?" Renee asked.

She shrugged. "My other reasons are still true, but yeah, that is part of it. I know it may seem like I'm running away…"

"No, it doesn't," Renee murmured. "If I had to do it again, I wouldn't have screwed up Jason's and my relationship with sex. Once you cross that line, there is no going back. My advice? Don't tell him, and just move on like you've planned."

"But you don't know it won't work out," Sophia softly interjected, even as she gave Renee's shoulder a gentle squeeze. "You're older, and in different places in your lives. You two could be different. But you'll never know if you're not honest with Dom. Believe me, if anyone has learned that keeping things from a person will only blow up in your face, I have."

"I appreciate both of you, I do." Though the conversation had taken a sobering turn, she was thankful to be able to call the two women friends. Hell, family. "But tonight I'd prefer not to think about Dom or men in general."

Sophia grinned. "Fine by me."

"Me, too," Renee agreed, though Tennyson detected the lingering sadness in her green eyes.

At that moment, their waitress arrived with their next round of drinks balanced on her tray. As she set the glasses on the table, Tennyson plucked hers up and held it in the air.

"Now, let's commence with the business of getting fucked up."

• • •

Dom shut off the television in the den, and, groaning, pushed himself to his feet and carefully stretched. Yesterday's game had been brutal, and he still bore some of the bruises and definitely the pain. He'd endured worse, but the loss to Atlanta seemed to make the aches scream louder than usual.

That and knowing every defeat was like another boulder added to the already stumbling weight on his shoulders. He'd let his team, coaches, and the fans down. Yeah, football was a team sport, but as the quarterback, he led them, was accountable for and to them. Each loss was a personal failure. God, he hated failure.

And not to mention, every time he missed a receiver or threw an interception, he could feel Jensen breathing down his neck, waiting for the opportunity to capitalize on Dom's fuck-ups. It wasn't the first time he'd had to battle for his position, and it wouldn't be the last. All his focus should be on their upcoming game against Buffalo, on perfecting his performance. But for the last few hours, instead of studying his play book and film of the Bills' past games, he'd been staring at his iPad and seeing Tenny, not players crashing into each other.

Something had happened between them earlier. Something he couldn't pinpoint or name.

For a second there, as they'd sat on the couch, glaring at each other over her insistence on meeting up with a perfect stranger, he thought he'd glimpsed arousal in her eyes. Which was ridiculous, impossible. There'd never been anything between them but the closest friendship. Well, except for that time when she'd been drunk and claimed to want him. But that had been the alcohol talking. Tenny had said so the next morning.

And yet...yet, he knew a woman's body, her mannerisms, the signs she gave off when she wanted to fuck him. He might avoid relationships like they were Egyptian plagues, but that didn't mean he didn't have years of experience. And for a moment, he'd believed the flush along her high cheekbones, the parting of her soft, full lips, the quick rise and fall of her pretty breasts...

Shit.

Wait. Wait, wait, *wait*.

Soft lips? Pretty breasts? He dragged a hand through his hair, fisting the strands at the back of his head. The pull and slight sting along his scalp served as a punishment and reminder. This was *Tennyson*. He didn't—couldn't—think of her like that.

Like what? A woman? He shook his head. As if the abrupt motion could rock loose the snide, insidious thought. The conversation with Zeph and Ronin must still be bothering him. That was the only explanation.

As if conjured by the force of his denial, an image of her flickered and solidified. Her, standing across the room in the black shirt, painted-on jeans, and high-heeled ankle boots that made her already toned, tight legs appear even more toned and tight. Petite, with breasts that would fill a man's hands, a tiny waist, and an ass that on any other woman would've had him panting, Tenny possessed the perfect hourglass figure. And though the outfit she'd worn damn near covered her from neck to toe, it'd still highlighted every curve, every dip, every sensual detail. Hell, he hadn't even been able to stop his gaze from dropping to the deeper-than-he-was-comfortable-with neckline of her top and taking in all that honeyed wheat flesh and its shadowed cleft. If she'd been anyone else, he would've wondered if that mysterious valley carried the heavier, muskier scent of her skin. He would've begged to find out...with his tongue.

But she wasn't someone else, goddamn it. She was his best friend, the person he trusted most in this world. And no way in hell would he jeopardize that precious gift with sex. He'd seen for himself the wreckage getting naked and sweaty with a friend left behind. They all had. Jason and Renee's shitstorm had made his entire circle of friends swear to keep their hands off one another. In this business where a smile could be a precursor to a knife in the back, players needed good, trustworthy friends. They were as priceless as a perfect season. And sometimes as rare.

Still, the hands-off-friends pact was moot. Because he didn't want to fuck Tennyson. Didn't see her as a woman to sink so deep into he'd need a fucking treasure map to find his way back out. A woman to drag screams from. A woman to make explode in pleasure and convulse around his cock.

No, he didn't want that with her.

And when he went upstairs and lay on his bed, it wouldn't be her face he envisioned as he pumped his dick into his fist.

"Shit," he muttered, stalking from the den. This was crazy; he must be more tired than he thought. His phone vibrated against his thigh, and he silently thanked whoever called for the interruption of the Tilt-a-Whirl his brain had obviously jumped on. Removing the cell from his shorts pocket, he glanced at the caller ID screen and frowned. Swiping the answer bar, he pressed the phone to his ear. "Hey, Sophia."

"Hi, Dom," Zeph's girlfriend greeted him. "I hate to bother you this late, but can you come to your front door?"

What the hell? But even as the question pulsed in his head, he'd already turned toward the foyer. An alarm set up in his chest, blinking its red caution with every heartbeat. "What's wrong? Is it Zeph?" The two had only been together a few months, but they were inseparable. And if she was at Dom's door at almost midnight...

"Uh, no. It's..." But he didn't hear the rest of her explanation because he'd reached the front of the house and, after quickly disarming the security system, jerked the door open.

Oh God.

Fear punched past alarm, throttling toward his throat. Sophia stood in the doorway. And Tenny leaned on her shoulder, head down. Jesus, was she hurt? What happened? He needed to call...

Tenny's head popped up, a huge grin lighting up her face. "Hiiiiii!" she sang, waving, as if he could miss her standing less than a foot in front of him. Slowly, panic released him from its icy claws, and relief rushed in, irritation fast on its heels.

She wasn't injured. Just shit-faced.

"Sophia," he growled, not removing his attention from his best friend and her glassy eyes. "What. The. Fuck?"

The other woman shrugged, smiling. "Margaritas followed by tequila shots." She shifted, tightening her hold around Tenny's shoulders. Sophia was a tall woman, but supporting drunken dead weight had to be tiring.

"You've got to be kidding me," he grumbled, reaching for Tenny. Gently, he slid his arm around her waist, easing her into his side.

"Sorry to just show up here," Sophia apologized, following them inside the foyer. "I tried to take her to my house, but she insisted on going home. I couldn't leave her alone like this, so I brought her here. I hope you don't mind."

Mind? Hell no. Tenny was wasted, and anything could happen if she was left alone at her apartment. And besides, his house was as much hers as his.

As if just realizing where she stood, Tenny straightened, her head swinging from side to side, then up and down. "Hey, this isn't my place," she complained, whirling around to face Sophia. Cursing, he grabbed her waist before she could tumble back on her ass. "You tricked me," she slurred, pointing a finger at Sophia. Or rather, to the left of her.

The other woman snorted. "Those tequila shots can have you seeing double. Well," she said, backpedaling toward the door. "I have to get Renee home."

"I'm guessing she's not as bombed," Dom drawled, once more wrapping an arm around Tenny, steadying her.

"Now that woman can hold her liquor. Although, she has

been singing Broadway show tunes the whole ride out here. When we got out of the car, she was on 'Defying Gravity' from *Wicked*. Night." Laughing, she left, closing the door behind her.

Sighing, Dom tucked Tenny closer under his shoulder and slowly turned her toward the staircase. Tequila and the citrus-scented shampoo she'd used for years drifted up to him, and the protective streak that had been forged in their childhood squeezed his chest in a vise-like grip. Since his parents' death, he and God had an understanding: he didn't bother God, and God didn't bother him. Yet, Dom couldn't deny it hadn't been a mistake Tenny had been brought to the same home as him. They'd been meant to be in each other's lives.

She was his to protect, to ensure the ugliness in this world didn't touch her again. Hell, she'd suffered enough of it with a mother—and he used the term loosely—who'd sought attention and sympathy by fabricating sickness symptoms and diagnoses in her own daughter. Tenny had been through hell, carted from doctor to doctor, enduring unnecessary test after test, even a surgery. All so her mother could get her psychological and emotional high. Psychiatrists called it Munchausen syndrome by proxy; he called it crazy as fuck.

It was this desire to shelter her that had him balking at her leaving him. He hadn't been able to protect his parents from a fatal car crash on their way to one of his Pop Warner football games. Yeah, he got that the accident wasn't his fault, but it didn't stop him from this almost desperate, visceral need to shield Tenny, to keep her close.

Hell, maybe he was the crazy one.

"I had the best time," she gushed, breaking into his thoughts. She didn't drink often—he could count on one hand how many times, including one very memorable instance—and, he'd never seen her this wasted. She was apparently a chatty drunk. A loud, chatty drunk. "Girls' Night Out. It should be a thing. Is it a thing? If not, it *totally* should be a thing."

"I think it's a thing. Hence the naming of it," he said drily, continuing to guide her toward the stairs. Damn, getting her up those steps wasn't going to be fun. At all.

"I had the best time," she crowed.

"You said that," he muttered, shuffling her forward.

"I always learn something new from Renee and Sophia. Like margaritas are God's way of saying 'I love you.'" She smacked her lips, humming. "And did you know that dicks could bend to the left?"

Dom stumbled. "Fuck."

"Doesn't that sound like it hurts?" she blathered on. "Does yours bend? I never noticed."

She started to look down, but gritting his teeth, he cupped her chin so her glassy gaze met his.

Oh for fuck's sake.

"Tennyson," he growled, hauling her up into his arms. *Screw this*. She shrieked in his ear, throwing her arms around his neck. "I swear to God I'm going to get Renee and Sophia back for this," he threatened, climbing the steps.

"Noooo," she objected, drawing the word out until it stretched into three syllables. "They're the only ones happy for me. Not like you," she groused, snuggling into his chest.

She turned so her breasts pressed against him, and shit, he couldn't stop himself from glancing down himself. Her flesh pillowed out of the deep V of her top, giving him a glimpse of the lacy edge of her black bra. That silken, golden skin rimmed in midnight lace—innocence wrapped in sin. *Jesus Christ*. He didn't pray, but it didn't stop him from calling on the deity for strength to tear his too-damn-fascinated scrutiny away from her.

Cursing, he took the rest of the stairs two at a time.

Once he hit the second floor landing, he rushed down the hall toward the room he'd appointed hers. Bumping his hip against the partially closed door, he charged inside and dropped her to the bed. As soon as he released her, he took a step back. Damn that. Two steps.

Tenny didn't seem to notice his reaction, instead falling back on the mattress and spreading her limbs wide like a snow angel. She sighed, her lashes lowering. Several minutes passed, and she didn't stir. Had she fallen off to sleep that fast?

"Tenny." He risked inching closer.

"Hmm." She didn't open her eyes.

"I'll be right back. Don't move." When she didn't reply, he heaved a sigh that could've parted the Red Sea. "Wiggle a finger if you hear me."

She wiggled two.

Taking that as an assent, he hurried down the stairs to the kitchen for a big glass of water, then to the master bedroom's bathroom for a bottle of aspirin. Moments later, he hustled back toward Tenny's room. God, please let her be awake. He shook his head as he neared her door. Trying to drag her out of a dead sleep when she was sober was like wrestling a feral cat. Wasted, it would probably be like wrestling a litter of them—

Fuuuuuuck.

His shoulder hit the doorjamb, but the jarring pain faded beneath the white noise that rushed into his head in a crashing wave. Shock tore through him, and his fingers tightened on the glass and bottle in his hands, damn near crushing both.

She'd obeyed his order and remained on the bed. But maybe he should've added "Keep your clothes on," because between the time he'd left her and now, she'd gotten rid of her shirt, jeans, and boots. Christ, she had the body of a goddess. Back before thin, small-chested women became the epitome of beauty, she would've been painted on murals and canvases. All those curves and soft skin would've been worshipped.

Black lace and silk cupped her gorgeous beasts, lifting them high as if offering them for a gentle caress, and not-so-soft gentle pinch. A long, savoring taste. The same material slid high over her hips and dipped to stroke between her legs, covering her...hiding her from him. Air whistled in and out of his lungs as if he'd just run ten gassers back-to-back at full speed. Every liter of blood in his body raced south to fill his cock.

Until this moment, he didn't know he'd wanted to discover if her sex would be the *café au lait* tone that covered the rest of her body. Would tight curls the same dark brown, almost black shade of her hair shield her, or would her folds be bare and glistening with arousal? Would her light scent of sun-warmed breezes and fresh rain be more condensed, headier between those toned, rounded thighs? Goddamn, he wanted to find out for himself.

He stumbled back a step. From her and the last blasphemous thought that had just run through his lust-hazed mind.

Lust. For Tennyson. It was...wrong. About fifteen different kinds of fucked up.

He'd seen his friend in a bathing suit before. How was this any different? His cock jerked behind his shorts. Right. He'd hadn't sprouted a hard-on then. *That's* how it was different.

Closing his eyes, he blocked out the sensual sight of his best friend in bra and panties. His *best friend*. Contrary to popular belief, he wasn't led around by his dick. It'd been three weeks since he'd gotten laid. Between Tennyson announcing her intentions to leave, being busy with football, and worrying over his performance, he'd been abstinent much longer than usual. That had to be the reason why he stood here wondering how her clit would quiver and flinch under his tongue.

Tomorrow. Tomorrow his number-one priority was getting a woman under him. Then this momentary...lapse would be an aberration that had never happened.

Clenching his jaw, he straightened from the doorjamb and entered the room, forcing his gaze to remain above her shoulders. "Tenny," he called. When she didn't move, he tried again, louder, adding more of a bark to his voice. "Tennyson."

Still nothing. He was going to have to touch her.

FML.

Setting the glass and bottle on the bedside table, he leaned over, eyes still trained on her face, and shook her shoulder. Ignoring the silken skin under his fingers. "Tennyson," he growled, not a little anger at himself roughening the tone.

"Huh?" Her lashes fluttered before finally lifting. "What happened?"

In spite of the confusion and irritation swirling in his chest, the corner of his mouth kicked up. She might be completely shit-faced, but God, she was cute.

"Sit up, babe." He retrieved the glass and aspirin. Popping the cap open, he shook three of the pills onto his palm. "Take these and drink the water. All of it. You'll thank me in the morning."

Groaning, she sat up. "Don't call me that," she grumbled, accepting the tablets.

"Don't call you what?" he asked, when she'd swallowed the medicine. "All of it," he reminded her, nodding at the water still remaining in the glass.

"Babe. That's what you call all your women."

He stared at her, speechless, as she downed the rest of the drink. Did he...? Maybe. But what did it matter to her? Better yet, *why* did it matter?

"I'm tired." The weariness in her voice snapped his attention back to her, and wordlessly, he took the glass and rounded the bed. Tugging the top blanket and sheet back, he waited as she crawled up the mattress.

Crawled.

This time he couldn't stop his gaze from sweeping the elegant slope of her spine or the firm, full flesh of her ass. Smothering a growl, he briefly closed his eyes, shutting out the carnal image. But it was branded on the back of his lids. Taunting him. Turning his dick into a steel spike.

Only when he heard her settle down did he risk looking down at her again. Desperate to cover all that skin, he pulled the blanket up to her shoulders.

"It's hot in here," she said, shoving the covers to her waist.

Well, that explained why she'd stripped. But, considering he had the air-conditioning on, it was probably the tequila talking. Sighing, he turned. That he felt like he'd just gone five rounds with Tyson Fury didn't escape him.

"I told Sophia not to bring me here," Tenny whispered. "I didn't want to come to your house."

He halted, surprise and not a little hurt flashing through him. "Why not?" he demanded, a part of him recognizing the wrongness of interrogating a drunk woman when the odds were she wouldn't remember a damn thing that had gone down the next morning. Including any confessions.

"Because."

He waited for her to continue. But all he got was a soft, little snore. His fingers curled into his palms, and he resisted the urge to shake her awake and answer his question. Instead he went to the bathroom, refilled the glass, and set it on the bedside table. Then he left, quietly closing the door behind him.

Yeah, suddenly, he didn't want to hear the answer.

Chapter Five

God, if You love me, please take me out now.

Tennyson moaned, rolling over. Or tried to. When her head threatened to explode into a bajillion pieces, she stopped moving. And deeply inhaled. Then gagged on her own breath that tasted somewhere between unwashed butt crack and hairy, unwashed butt crack. Yech. Though her lashes seemed fused together with superglue, she lifted them and whimpered, immediately regretting her decision. So that's how Scott Summers, aka Cyclops, felt when fire erupted from his eyes. Huh.

Sometime later—maybe minutes, hours, days—she awoke again. The sunlight pouring into the room from the window across from her didn't pierce her eyeballs like thousands of needles, so she must feel a little better than the first time she'd attempted to lift her lids. Her breath could still choke a fire-breathing dragon, though.

Moaning, she gingerly shifted until she sat on the edge of the bed. The room didn't spin, and only contracted and expanded once. Progress. Slowly, she glanced around.

Wait. This wasn't her apartment.

How did she end up at Dom's house?

As if the question twisted the knob on the door to her memory, fragments from the previous evening started to trickle through the fog encasing her brain.

Margaritas. Tequila shots. Sing-a-long of "Circle of Life." Trying to size up Dom's dick.

Oh Jesus H. Christ.

Slapping a palm over her eyes, she groaned. What had she done?

Cool air whispered over her bare shoulders and chest. Wait. Bare shoulders and chest...

What in the hell happened to her clothes?

As if only too happy to supply the answers, her mind flashed an image of her stripping and falling onto the bed in her bra and panties. Followed by a picture of Dom standing over her.

Had she asked God to take her out? No, she now needed Him to obliterate her in a bolt of lightning so nothing of her humiliated carcass remained.

Never again. She was never touching another drop of alcohol again.

Dragging herself to her feet, she inched along toward the bathroom. Forty-five minutes later, she emerged from the bedroom, showered, dressed in a T-shirt and yoga pants, and damp hair in a messy top bun. Claiming to feel human was a stretch, but at least microwaved death was no longer an option.

Gripping the railing, she crept down the staircase, following the mouthwatering aroma of frying bacon. An hour ago, she wouldn't have believed she'd crave anything to eat, but now her stomach rumbled for food. And not just any food. Bacon.

Entering the kitchen, she spotted Dom at the stove in his

customary day-off outfit—T-shirt, low-hanging sweatpants, and bare feet. His muscles rippled and danced under the shirt's tight cotton as he cooked. The tousled, wavy hair brushed his solid jaw, and that quick, she was jealous of the dark brown strands. Her fingertips itched to trace the stubborn line up to the carnal, full bottom lip.

She shook her head. "Damn," she muttered, clutching at her temples. That had been a *huge* mistake.

Dom glanced up and over his shoulder. She forced herself to meet his gaze, apprehension over what she would find there skittering through her. Though she recalled some of her behavior the night before, she still didn't remember everything. And God knows what else she'd done or said. Nerves cramped her belly. Well, God knew, and so did Dom.

Jesus, the last time she'd been around him drunk had scarred her and caused friction in their relationship. One would think she'd have learned her lesson.

But as she stared into his eyes, she didn't see speculation, anger, or—thank the Lord—pity. She obviously hadn't revealed anything...like how much she wanted him more than bacon.

"I'm guessing you're feeling okay since you're vertical," he greeted with an arch of his eyebrow.

She grimaced, moving farther into the room and carefully sitting on one of the chairs at the large oval breakfast table.

"'Okay' would be optimistic," she said. "I'm alive. I think."

He returned to scrambling eggs and flipping bacon. "That means the aspirin helped."

"Yeah, thanks for that and...everything." The words came out sounding more like a question than a statement, since she was uncertain what "everything" actually entailed.

He shot her a look and snorted. "Now who has the faulty forgettery?"

"Very funny," she grumbled. "Speaking of last night..."

"Yeah?"

"Did I...do anything I need to apologize for?" she hedged.

He flicked off the burner knobs and turned to fully face her, arms crossed over his chest. "Like what?"

"Dom," she moaned.

"You mean like scaring the hell out of me by showing up wasted out of your mind? Or do you mean trying to check out my dick to find out what direction it pointed?" he suggested.

Oh hell.

"Or maybe you're talking about passing out on me?" he added.

Wincing, she lifted a shoulder in an apologetic shrug. "Sorry. If it's any consolation, I've already sworn not to get drunk ever again."

Silently, she sighed in relief. He hadn't mentioned her ending up in her underwear. Maybe she'd undressed herself after he put her to bed...

"Or do you mean stripping down to your bra and panties and flashing your tits at me?"

She gasped, her head jerking up. Ignoring the protesting throbbing in her temples, she gaped at him. "I didn't."

He arched that damn eyebrow again. "Strip?"

"Flash my breasts at you," she whispered, mortified. Oh hell, had she? She couldn't remem—

"I'm kidding," he chuckled. "No flashing."

"Asshole." But the relief coursing through her stole the fire from the insult.

Still laughing, he piled food on two plates and brought them to the table. The next few minutes, a comfortable silence reigned between them as they tucked into the pretty decent eggs, bacon, and toast. When she'd had her fill, he reached over and scooped the rest of her food onto his plate.

Business as usual.

"What're your plans for the day?" He pushed away from the table and, moments later, returned with two mugs of coffee, hers with cream and no sugar just the way she liked it.

"Nothing much for the morning and afternoon, but you have a lunch date scheduled with Brian at eleven thirty," she said, naming his agent. "And a telephone interview with *Maxim* at two. Followed by a four o'clock meeting at your attorney's to sign the final contract for the shoe endorsement." She eyed him over the rim of her coffee cup. "I uploaded it all into your phone's calendar."

"So much for a day off." He leaned back in his chair. "You want to come with me to meet Brian?"

She shook her head, scrunching up her nose. "He's a cool guy, but he has this bad habit of talking to my boobs. No thanks."

At the mention of the part of her anatomy that had been the bane of her existence since she turned twelve, his gaze dropped, and she froze, her coffee cup halfway to the table. Something flashed across his face—something too quick to identify—but her heart stuttered, then started pounding against her rib cage.

"Dom?"

He picked up his mug and drank from it, not answering her but studying the brew inside the cup as if it held the day's lottery numbers.

"I didn't know he made you uncomfortable," he finally said, standing and collecting their plates. Not once did he meet her eyes. Unease slid through her. "I'll talk to him about it. Or is there something you're not telling me? I can fire him."

"No, nothing terrible, other than wandering eyes. I don't want to cause any trouble," she murmured, turning in her chair. "Dom," she hesitated. "Are you sure nothing else happened last night?"

"I'm sure." He rinsed the dishes and loaded them in the dishwasher. She frowned, the disquiet not easing. But before she could question him further, he said, "You mentioned you have nothing planned for this morning and afternoon. So you got something going this evening?"

Well, damn. She hated lying to him...

No, she didn't. "Nope."

"You know you can't lie for shit, right?" Eyes narrowed, he scrutinized her, and she met it with a carefully innocent expression. Just in case, she widened her eyes a bit more, and he snorted in disgust. "Please."

"What?" She stood from the table and headed toward the kitchen entrance. "I have to get going. Give me a ride home?"

Her fast movement jarred her head and sent the dull throb to full on Thor's-Hammer-Against-the-Skull. But better to deal with the headache than admit that she had plans to meet Adam tonight. She just wasn't having that discussion with Dom.

"Fine." Pause. "Then we can finish our conversation."

"I'll call an Uber."

"I wouldn't dream of it," came his cheerful reply. As if that jovial tone could hide the steel beneath it.

She rolled her eyes and continued up the stairs. No doubt he planned to try to get more information about her plans out of her. But she had avoidance down to a fine art.

She'd been a master at it for years.

Chapter Six

Adam Rutheridge was everything he'd claimed on his dating profile.

Tall, a little on the slender side, but still cute in that intellectual, Clark Kent way. Black-rimmed glasses; spiky hair with an undercut; conservatively dressed in a sports coat, dress shirt, and khakis with another of those adorable bowties—this time tiny sleeping blue kittens against a brick-red background. Hip but not too preppy. Nice. Polite. Attentive.

And so damn boring, she was about to fake choking on her antipasto so she could escape. Only the thought of the ambulance bill kept her from grabbing for her throat and falling out in a violent, paroxysmal fit.

But if he regaled her once more with tales of how his brilliant British Blue Shorthair Charlie could play "Chopsticks" on Adam's baby grand piano, she would consider the money well spent.

She'd had such high hopes for HappilyEverAdam. Had made dinner reservations for them at Assagio's, one of the best restaurants in Seattle. She should know, since she'd arranged for Dom to take his dates here often enough. But no such luck. Looks like she would be repurposing the short, form-fitting black cocktail dress she'd bought specifically for this date. She eyed the tiny cup of Italian salad dressing next to her plate. Spilling it on the gorgeous dress would be a shame, but…

"I've had Charlie since she was a kitten. Bought her when I lived in New York, and we've been together ever since. I'm thinking about getting another cat to keep her company since I'm now traveling a lot for my job as a pharmaceutical rep. But," he chuckled, shrugging and adjusting his glasses on the bridge of his nose. "What are the odds of finding another cat who can play 'Chopsticks'…"

"Right," she absently agreed, reaching for the dressing. The little black number would be taking one for the team…

"Wow, what a coincidence. Fancy meeting you here, Tenny." She froze, Dom's familiar voice aborting her wardrobe emergency.

Shock socked the air from her lungs, and she could only stare in confusion and disbelief at the sight of her friend standing next to her table. She blinked. Stared some more. Nope, she wasn't imagining him. Or the statuesque redhead in the tiny gold dress, either.

Son. Of. A. Bitch.

On second thought, that wasn't really fair to his mother.

Bastard.

"What are you doing here?" she blurted, finally finding her voice.

"*OMG*," Adam blurted out at the same time, gawking at Dom. "Dominic Anderson! I can't believe it!" he practically yelled. Apparently, Adam had one more interest besides his cat's musical tastes. Football. Greeeaaat.

Dom turned to her, and the fall of his hair hid his face

from everyone but her as he mouthed, "OMG." His irritating smirk tightened a bit at the corners of his mouth as his gaze dropped down and skated over her bare shoulders and the deep V of her dress. What a hypocrite. He had the nerve to be disapproving while his date's hem played hide and seek with her hoo-haa. As quick as the look of displeasure appeared, it vanished by the time he turned and stretched a hand toward Adam, replaced by the charming grin that'd had several toothpaste companies calling, begging to have him be the face of their brand. Thoroughly captivated—or snowed— Adam rose from the table, his chair screeching across the floor in his haste. But he didn't seem to notice as he grabbed Dom's hand and pumped it with the excitement Tennyson had assumed he reserved only for his British Blue.

"Nice to meet you..." Dom paused, and Adam delightedly filled in the space.

"Adam. Adam Rutheridge."

"Nice to meet you, Adam." Dom turned to his date, a hand settled on the small of her back. Tennyson tried *really* hard not to resent her for the small, solicitous touch. "This is Julia Rowland. Julia, Adam Rutheridge and Tennyson Clark."

"Ooh. How cute," Julia cooed. "*A Streetcar Named Desire* is one of my favorite films."

A Streetcar Named... Hell. "Actually," Tennyson said, struggling to not fall out of her chair and roll on the floor laughing, "that's Tennessee Williams. I'm named after the poet, Alfred, Lord Tennyson." At the other woman's blank stare, Tennyson lifted a shoulder in a half shrug. "'Maud' and 'The Kraken'?" Nothing. "'Charge of the Light Brigade?' *Into the valley of Death rode the...* Never mind."

"No worries, Julia. People make that mistake all the time," Dom assured his date. And didn't once glance down at Tennyson as he uttered the blatant lie. "Hey, how about we join you two?"

Damn. She'd *known* it was coming.

"I'm sure you and Julia—" she began.

"That would be amazing," Adam crowed, interrupting and overriding her.

You can't punch him in the throat. You can't punch him in the throat.

As if by magic, two waiters appeared with extra chairs that they settled on either side of her. Dom lowered in the seat to her left, while his date sat in the one on Tennyson's right. A pout turned her crimson lips downward. Probably because she couldn't cuddle next to Dom during the meal. It seemed Tennyson wasn't the only one eating a healthy serving of disappointment tonight.

"What are you doing here?" she asked Dom again.

"Dinner, obviously." He cocked his head. "You more than anyone should know it's one of my favorite restaurants."

Yes, she did, but he hadn't mentioned anything about a date tonight. And she scheduled all his meetings—including dates, and there had been nothing entered in. She'd double-checked before choosing this restaurant. The coast should've been clear, but no. Fate and life hated her.

"Right," she agreed, and couldn't help that the word emerged sounding like she choked on it.

"Sooo." Adam glanced from her to Dom, fidgeting with the frame of his glasses. Again. "You two obviously know each other."

She slid a look at Dom, and he winked at her. The fall of sleek, dark brown waves framed his chiseled cheekbones and wide, carnal mouth. The amusement in his eyes only made them appear bluer.

Damn, the man was beautiful.

Before he'd arrived, the round table she and Adam shared had seemed small, but with just enough space for them. But

Dom's giant, wide-shouldered frame dwarfed everything—the table, her, Adam. His thick thigh pressed against hers, and a fantasy image of those same heavy legs widening hers as he crushed her body to a bed swamped her. She tried to suck in a deep breath, but his presence that brimmed with energy and sexuality seemed to vacuum the air from the entire restaurant, overwhelming their mismatched foursome. Poor Adam, with his perfectly handsome features, trendy glasses, and clothes, didn't stand a chance against him.

"Yes," she agreed, forcing a smile. She hated that she was once more comparing a man to Dom. And the other man fell short. "We're childhood friends. More like brother and sister," she added, more for her own benefit than her date's. The reminder would serve to usher the erotic vision of her and Dom out of her head.

"Well, I don't know about that," Dom drawled. "I mean, I've never seen my sister in her underwear."

Did he just…? Oh shit, he did. She gaped at him. "Y-you don't even have a s-sister," she sputtered, caught between outrage and shock. Which explained the completely inane comeback.

Though he nodded solemnly, a wicked gleam brightened his eyes. "True. But if I did, I doubt she would take off her clothes in front of me."

Adam's gasp had her head snapping back toward her date. For the time being, she opted to ignore Julia's snort that reeked of disapproval. Since she probably had every intention of stripping for Dom later that night, she really shouldn't be a judgy bitch.

"He's not telling the whole story," she hurriedly explained to Adam, who regarded her and Dom with wide eyes and parted lips. "It isn't as bad as it sounds."

"Again, true," Dom added, his tone helpful. All kinds of *oh fuck* trickled through her. "She was wasted at the time," he stage-whispered.

She briefly closed her eyes. Yes, she'd been about to abandon the date with Adam before Dom showed up. But that would've been *her* decision, not a result of Dom's interference. And she'd rather Adam not leave thinking she was a lush.

"It was a girls' night out," she ground out between clenched teeth, trying a reassuring smile with Adam. But from his flinch, it must've appeared more like a feral baring of teeth. Because it definitely felt like it.

"Yes, a girls' night out," Dom recited, a wealth of *That's her story, and I'm sticking to it*, all up in the words. "She's not a drunk."

He shifted her half-filled glass of wine closer to him.

Dead.

He was so dead.

And as Adam lifted a hand and signaled for the check, apparently so was this date.

• • •

Dom punched a code into the keypad next to the large, black, iron gate that served as the front entrance to Tennyson's Kirkland private community. Impatient, he waited until the gates swung open the minimum required amount of space before driving through. He barely noticed the well-maintained and beautifully kept townhomes and apartments. When Tenny had first toured the area, she'd fallen in love with the small neighborhood feel of it with the towering trees and so much…green. Dom had liked it because of the security system. Twenty-four-hour guards. Cameras covering every section of the complex—he'd checked. State-of-the-art alarm systems in the individual units. If she refused to stay with him, then he'd wanted to ensure she had the best protection possible.

Still, as he pulled into a guest parking space and climbed the steps to her second-floor apartment, he doubted all that security would shield him from the Wrath of Tennyson. Not after his performance at the restaurant earlier. He winced. Yeah, he might have gone a little overboard with the alcoholic insinuation. And her death glare as she'd stalked away from him promised retribution. Painful retribution. But hopefully, the hour and a half it'd taken to disentangle himself from Julia and make his excuses before dropping her off at home had provided Tennyson with enough time to cool off.

Or, at least, enough time where she would no longer want to inflict bodily harm.

Sighing, he reached her front door and knocked. And waited. Knocked again. Waited some more. Still no answer.

He knew Tenny better than anyone. And the woman had a heart the size of the Atlantic, but when she got angry, she could hold it until the damn cows came home, left, ventured on a whirlwind vacation, and returned again. Since he only had one life to live, he'd rather let her get this fury out of her system now, and then they could move on.

Inserting his emergency key to her place into her front door, he unlocked it and, like he had thousands of times before, let himself in. Silence greeted him. The television that continually remained on whenever she was home sat dark in the enormous entertainment center he and Zeph had put together. Only the light over the stove and the pale glow from the streetlamps peeking through the slats of the closed blinds provided dim illumination of the spacious living and dining rooms. This early in October, the wide fireplaces in both rooms remained unlit.

He roamed through the rest of the apartment, finding the guest bedroom and bathroom empty. Just as he neared her bedroom, he caught a faint sound. Pausing, he identified the low drum as water. Shower water. Relieved that Tenny was home safe, he returned to the living room, switched on the television, and settled on the couch.

But part of him was attuned to the sound of water pounding against tile upstairs instead of *SportsCenter*. Focused on the image of wet, slick, golden skin. And when the shower stopped, his mind immediately conjured up a corresponding vision. That same skin, flushed and smooth, patted dry with one of the same kind of fluffy towels Tennyson kept in her room at his house. He tightened his grip on the remote, shoving the sensual pictures from his head where they definitely didn't belong. Hell, maybe he shouldn't have been so quick to take Julia home. Maybe he should've accepted her invitation, stayed, and fucked away this completely inappropriate preoccupation with his best friend.

Still, when her bedroom door opened, he was aware of every movement.

"What the hell are you doing here?" The snapped question interrupted Scott Van Pelt discussing the upcoming Denver vs. Seattle game but didn't surprise him. He casually turned, but the light-hearted reply he had ready died a swift death on his tongue.

Damn.

He'd thought the black dress she'd worn to dinner, with its figure-hugging material and deep neckline that revealed the inner curves of her breasts, had been bad. Bad as in barely checking his urge to yank the white tablecloth off and throw it around her like a reverse cape. But that dress didn't compare to Tennyson standing several feet away in a purple robe that hit her mid-thigh. The silk clung to several damp spots on her shoulder, chest, and legs. And he couldn't tear his gaze away from them. Couldn't stop imagining how slick the wet material would feel under his fingertips.

"Since you have televisions at your house, I'm guessing you're not here to just watch *SportsCenter*," she drawled, crossing her arms under her breasts. A groan climbed up his throat. The movement caused the lapels of her robe to slightly gap, exposing a sliver of skin that wasn't hindered by a bra clasp. *Jesus Christ.* Of all his bad mistakes in life, his decision to show up here unannounced had now zoomed into the top five.

"Dom, hello? What're you doing here?" she repeated, arching an eyebrow.

"I have a key," he said, holding up his ring.

"A. That's an emergency key. Which means unless you see flames pouring from my windows or my house falling into a crack because of shifting plates, then you don't just get to use it when I'm mad at you. And B. That doesn't answer my question. What do you want?"

Okay, this wasn't good. There'd always been an open-door policy between them. For her to revoke it meant she was royally pissed off. And probably not in the mood to hear how he was sorry to have crashed her date. That he'd made an impromptu date with Julia with every intention of dining and then ending up in her bed that night. But when he'd seen Tenny with that Adam guy, all his intentions to get laid had gone the way of the wooly mammoth. All he could think about was making sure she was safe meeting this complete stranger from an online dating site.

Besides, after he'd gotten a closer look at the guy, his intention had been to save her. HappilyEverAdam had definitely not been her type. Not that Dom could pinpoint what her "type" was since she rarely dated, but he could definitely say Dull as Fuck wasn't it. The guy had looked like he'd come straight from an episode of *The Big Bang Theory*. Since she probably wouldn't appreciate his opinion at the moment, he kept it to himself.

He stood and shoved his hands in the front pockets of his dress pants. "I wanted to apologize for tonight. I might've gone too far."

"Might have?" Her eyes narrowed on him. "You horned in on my date. Then you insinuated that I was a drunk who made a habit of stripping in front of people. I'd say there's no 'might have gone too far' about it," she snarled. "When was the last time I popped up in your bedroom, climbed up on the mattress, and plopped my ass in between you and one of your football groupies while you were trying to get your one-night stand on?" She jabbed a finger at him. "Have I ever followed you to one of your DTF starlets' houses, knocked on the door with a tray of milk and cookies, and proceeded to talk to her about her latest movie? I'll tell you when. Never."

Milk and cookies? He swallowed the snicker tickling the back of his throat.

"How did you find out where we were anyway?" she demanded.

He held his hands up. "Purely accidental, I swear. I should be asking you why you'd take your date to the same restaurant you know I frequent."

Maybe she'd subconsciously *wanted* him to horn in on her date... Yeeaah, that glare said differently. Actually, it said, *Go fuck yourself.*

"You didn't say anything about a date tonight," she pointed out. "It wasn't on your calendar. How was I supposed to know you'd show up and torpedo my first meeting with Adam to hell and back?"

He shrugged. "C'mon, Tenny. You were about to fake a heart attack or something to get out of that place. I saw it all over your face when I arrived."

"That's not the point. Oh, hell, never mind." She waved a hand. "Why, Dom? Your actions tonight just prove why I didn't tell you about my date. You can't help yourself, can you? Interfering in my life? Making my decisions for me? Deciding what's best for me?"

"That's not true," he objected, his own irritation starting to rise. She made him sound like some kind of control freak. Honestly, he didn't know what was wrong with him lately. Actually, he just cared about her—her welfare, her safety, her happiness. And granted, Adam, aka HappilyEverAdam, hadn't come across as the next serial killer to be featured on an ID Discovery special, but he damn sure wouldn't have made Tennyson happy. Hell, if Adam hadn't been so busy flapping his gums, he might have caught on to her boredom.

Dom wisely kept that observation to himself.

"But you know what?" she continued as if he hadn't spoken. "I only have myself to blame. Paying my college tuition, setting me up with a job, finding my apartment, even choosing my freakin' car insurance—I let you get away with it all because it was comfortable. It's what I've known for so long. Too long."

"What the hell are *you* talking about now?" Dom barked, striding across the several feet that separated them. "I did all that because we're family, not to control or manage you."

"We are *not* family," she replied, voice sharp. And those four words jabbed him in the chest, expelling all the air from his lungs. "I'm not the broken little girl from the foster home who you took under your wing anymore. No matter how much you still think I am."

"*Goddamn it*," he growled, getting up in her space. Anger shoved at him, ate at him. The hell he wanted her to be that eleven year-old with the wounded eyes and heart. It'd been his life's mission to make her forget what betrayal, pain, and hunger felt like. And here she stood, accusing him of... "If you think I want that for you, then you don't know me one fucking bit, Tennyson."

"No, you don't want me to be her, but you see me as that

girl. You're still trying to be my hero, my protector, my big brother. I don't need to be protected, and I damn sure don't want you as my brother. My life has revolved around yours for the last fourteen years. I want my own. I want to walk my own path. Make my own way. Without you hovering over my shoulder, trying to force me into the direction *you* think *I* should go for my own good. I'm tired of it," she stormed. "You don't respect me as an adult capable of making her own decisions—"

"Could you please stop for a minute?"

She complied, blinking up at him, probably shocked at his asking her to be quiet or the "please"—maybe both.

We are not family.

I don't need to be protected, and I damn sure don't want you as my brother.

You don't respect me…

Anger licked at him, burning him in its flames. Anger, frustration…hurt. They all propelled him forward. Before he could question himself—reason with himself—he was moving, pinning her to the wall, thrusting his fingers through her thick, nearly black curls. Pressing his chest to hers, grinding his cock into the soft give of her stomach. She didn't utter a word, just stared up at him, shock darkening her eyes, parting her lush lips.

"We're not family? You don't want me to protect you?" He hurled her words back at her, tightening his grip on her hair, pulling her head back just a little farther. Her lashes fluttered, and her breath caught, the soft gasp of air brushing his mouth. Oh hell. She liked that. Eyes narrowing on the flush that lightly colored her cheekbones, he tugged on her hair again, a little firmer than the last time. Once more, she gave another of those almost imperceptible pants, a small, *hungry* sound accompanying it. Her fingers curled into his shirt, her nails barely scraping his chest through the material.

But he felt the light scratch all the way in his dick as if she'd drawn them down his already throbbing erection.

Fuck.

Common sense railed at him to unravel his fingers from her hair, let her go, and back away. But lust had smothered reason as soon as he heard that greedy sound and sexy gasp. He'd always been mindful of his bigger frame and strength, and gentle in his interactions with her. But it seemed Tennyson liked it when he wasn't so...*gentle*. The knowledge sent a blaze of fire blasting through him.

"Dom," she whispered, her lashes lifting. Confusion shadowed her eyes. But so did arousal. And it was the heat there that had him pressing closer until she raised on her toes, another of those whimpers escaping her. Hell, he could make dragging that sound from her another career.

What are you doing? the rational side of his brain scolded. But he barely paid it any heed. The primal side of his psyche had taken hold. And screw it, he let it take over.

"Let me show you what I do to women who aren't *family*," he rasped.

He crushed his mouth to hers, not waiting, but thrusting his tongue between her lips. Her flavor exploded over his senses—the sweetness of the Riesling wine she'd had with dinner and a unique, earthier taste that he'd never sampled before but still somehow knew belonged only to her. With a deep groan, he tilted his head and delved deeper, claimed more of her with a carnal sweep.

Yet something—reason, instinct, the protective side of him he couldn't ever banish—cautioned him, reminded him that she wasn't just one of the women he casually fucked. Even as he rocked his cock into her belly and widened her thighs with his, he remembered this was Tennyson. And the hard possession of his mouth gentled just a bit. Became a little more tender. More sensual.

He licked at the roof of her mouth before curling his tongue around hers, inviting her to tangle with him. And she did. With bold strokes and strong sucks. With a hard nip to his bottom lip. His hips bucked at the sting, and he growled his approval, returning the favor.

Need clouded his head in a thick haze. Running on straight, pure lust, he released his grip on her hip and slid his hand over the dip of her waist, stroking up until he cupped her breast. He moaned at the weight of her. Firm. Feminine. Heavy. Lifting his head, he stared down, fierce pleasure barreling through him at the sight of her silk-covered flesh in his hand. Her nipple, hard and tight, poked his palm, and he squeezed the mound, shaped it. Swept his thumb over the tip.

She jerked against him, loosing a soft cry. Damn, he loved that sound. He flicked the peak, pinched it. And was rewarded with another of those needy cries. She arched into his hand, her body begging for more of what he could give her. Of what he *wanted* to give her. Lowering his head, he brushed his mouth over her jaw and traveled down the elegant line of her throat.

With a growl, he bent further, studied the steady pass of his thumb over the tightly beaded nipple thrusting against the silk of her robe. Unable to resist the lure of her aroused flesh, he captured the tip with his mouth, sucking it and the soft material deep inside. Her fingers tangled in his hair, her nails scratching his scalp. The tiny bite arrowed straight to his dick, and he ground harder against her...

"Dom," she breathed, her eyes glazed with the passion he'd caused.

Maybe it was the taut quality of her voice that jerked him from the erotic rabbit hole he'd tumbled down. Maybe it was his nosy-as-hell inner voice that whispered he needed to stop before he went too far. As if his tongue wrapped around his best friend's nipple wasn't *too far*.

"Damn it," he swore, low and hot. Wrenching himself away from her, he stumbled back a step before quickly regaining his balance. She stared at him, those dark brown eyes still hazy with desire, her full lips swollen from his hungry kisses, arousal staining her high, elegant cheekbones. Her robe, disheveled by his body and touch, gaped to expose the path of skin between her breasts.

The almost overwhelming need to return to her and shove that covering off her shoulders and take more of what he'd tasted tore through him like a destructive tornado. He whipped around, unable to continue looking at the image of tousled sexuality she presented. Burrowing all ten fingers in his hair, he clenched the strands in his fists.

What have I done? What was I thinking? The still-insistent ache in his dick assured him that he hadn't been *thinking* at all. Or if he had, not with the right head.

"I'm sorry," he murmured, still unable to face her. She was his friend—his best friend. And he'd treated her like one of the women he picked up for a night of fucking. Jumped on her. Ground his cock against her. Damn near shoved his tongue down her throat. How had he lost such control that he'd nearly damaged years of friendship? Had he learned *nothing*? He *had* to fix this. Turning to face her, he dropped his arms to his sides, met her now clearer gaze. "That shouldn't have happened. I shouldn't have touched you like that, Tenny. I know sorry is pathetic as hell, but I'm sorry," he repeated the apology.

Even as he acknowledged that, he still kept a physical distance between them.

She slowly straightened and pushed off the wall. Not immediately replying, she rearranged her robe, tightened the belt. And when she lifted her head, the arousal had disappeared, leaving behind a careful indifference that scraped at his nerves.

"No worries," she said, that same coolness in her voice. "Believe me, I know you didn't mean it." She pivoted and headed toward the hall. "I'm tired, so if you don't mind, I'm going to bed. You can let yourself out."

Without waiting for his response, she disappeared down the corridor.

Though part of him longed to follow her and reaffirm that things hadn't changed between them because of his momentary loss of control, he remained standing in the same spot until the click of her door reached him.

Only then did he leave. Going after her would've only spelled disaster.

She more than anyone should understand he didn't do relationships. But Tenny wasn't built for one-night stands, for casual sex. He couldn't ever give her what she wanted—what she deserved. And ignoring this glaring fact would only hurt and damage their relationship more.

Yeah, "more." Because no matter how much he wanted their relationship to remain the same, he knew it couldn't.

Now he just had to figure out how to set things right, how not to lose his best friend because of a kiss. A wild, hot-as-hell, prelude-to-fucking kiss.

Hell. He was screwed.

Chapter Seven

Tennyson paused in the middle of replying to an email, accepting request for an interview with Dom on ESPN in three weeks. She thought she'd heard... Yep, there it was. She must've turned her cell phone ringer off by mistake, but that was definitely her phone vibrating inside her purse.

Diving for her bag, she retrieved her phone, glancing at the caller ID screen. Not a number she recognized, but that wasn't exactly unusual. Many of Dom's business interests called her since, as his PA, she was the point of contact for him.

Still, she couldn't deny the trickle of relief that filtered through her when Dom's number didn't pop up. It'd been six days since her disastrous date with Adam. Six days since Dom showed up at her home.

Six days of distance and awkward politeness between them because of The Kiss.

Yes, The Kiss deserved to be capitalized like an event or battle that changed the course of history. Because it'd definitely altered their history. Hell, their present and possibly their future. Years ago, he'd told her there could never be more between them than a best friend relationship—he hadn't wanted more. And though he'd taken her mouth like a starving man, his apology and regret afterward had pretty much cemented that he still didn't. She could press him, ask what that kiss had been about. But she wasn't ashamed to admit she feared the answer.

Since that night, she'd opted to work from her apartment instead of his home office. And other than necessary discussions about business, they hadn't called each other to shoot the shit like they usually did. It was ironic—they avoided talking about The Kiss to avoid awkwardness. But not talking about it was awkward as hell.

Well, since she'd had more free time, at least she'd finally tried several new recipes, including one she found on Facebook for chicken enchilada zucchini boats. And a really delicious recipe from Sophia's mom for tembleque, a Puerto Rican coconut pudding dessert.

She'd also gone to her annual doctor's appointment. Those were hell for her. The office wasn't as terrifying as a hospital, but she still had to mentally prepare herself for days beforehand. They both had the same smell of disinfectant. The same sterile appearance. The same physicians and nurses with their instruments, needles, and questions... She shook her head and inhaled, focusing on calming her pulse. Yes, she could've called Dom and reminded him, and he undoubtedly would've come with her as he'd done in the past, holding her hand and sitting in the waiting room in case she needed him. But she had to learn to stand on her own two feet, especially since she'd applied for jobs out of state. In the future, he wouldn't be able to jump on a plane and go to an appointment with her.

And seriously, if she had reached out to him, what would she have said?

Hey, Dom. I know the last time we saw each other your dick was pressed into my stomach, but could you come with me to my doctor's appointment? Oh, and by the way, I've decided to add fire insurance to my policy, because that kiss set my panties ablaze!

Not that it wouldn't be the truth, because holy flame-retardant undies, it had been...combustible.

For those few moments, she'd been wanted, desired. By Dom the man, not her buddy. For that short span of time, he'd no longer regarded her as the fragile, delicate Tennyson who needed sheltering. And the hard, uncompromising press of his body to hers, the firm tug of her hair, the hard clasp of her hip had confirmed it. All of it had been stunning...and wickedly delicious.

Over the years, her mind had conjured up countless fantasies about how it would be if they finally crossed that friendship line. Those dreams had alternated between sweet and romantic to sexy and dirty. Never could she have imagined the reality would be a carnal combination of all four. Jesus, he'd...tongue-fucked her mouth. No other way to put it. And the solid, heavy weight of his cock against her... It'd been hot. And yet, there'd been tenderness in the teasing, indulgent licks and kisses.

But then, he'd jerked away as if scalded. And not in a good way.

That quick, he'd reminded her that she wasn't one of the women he pursued and bedded. Whatever had pushed him to kiss her—anger, frustration, hell, a bad burger on the way over to her house—had evaporated, leaving regret and horror at himself behind. He'd kissed and touched *her*. Tennyson, his friend whom he'd never shown the slightest interest in. Who could never attract him with her too-ripe curves, short stature, naïveté, and sisterly bonds.

Although that kiss had been faaarr from sisterly.

Stop it, she ordered herself. From the dismay that had filled his expression when he'd pulled himself away from her as if she were the clap, she knew that kiss would never be repeated.

Which, if she were honest, was probably a good thing. Before The Kiss—BTK—other men had failed miserably in comparison to him. ATK, it would be even harder for them to measure up. Anything more, and she might as well take vows and become a bride of Christ. Because she feared no man would have a chance of competing against the sexual power that was Dominic Anderson. And she *had* to move on. *Had* to make this new start. Tuesday night proved the urgency of it more now than ever.

Sighing, she swiped a thumb across the answer bar. "Tennyson Clark."

"Yes, Ms. Clark. This is Veronica Maitland with the Offices of Families and Children in Dayton, Ohio," the brisk, feminine voice on the other end greeted. "I'm calling about your application for the Child Welfare Caseworker 1 position. We received your résumé and would like to set up a convenient time for a telephone interview since you currently reside in Seattle."

Excitement edged with nervousness leaped inside her, and her grip on the phone tightened. "Thank you for contacting me, Ms. Maitland," she said. And even though her heart pounded so hard it felt like the organ had lodged itself in her throat, she congratulated herself on the calm tone. "As you probably noted on my résumé, I currently work as a personal assistant, so my schedule is flexible. When you have an opening, I'll make sure I'm available." God, she hoped that didn't sound desperate.

"Okay. Seattle is behind Dayton by two hours, so how about eleven o'clock this Thursday? That would be nine your time. Is that too early?" she asked.

"Not at all," Tennyson assured the other woman. "Nine on

Thursday. Sounds perfect." Oh my God. This was happening. That same queasy mixture of eagerness and anxiety churned in her belly.

"Great, I'll add it to my schedule now." The click of fingers tapping over a keyboard echoed across the line. "Do you mind if I ask you a question, Ms. Clark?"

"Not at all," Tennyson replied, hoping she didn't risk blowing her interview before it even happened.

"You currently live in Seattle. Why are you applying for a job in Dayton?"

Tennyson didn't immediately answer, formulating her response in her head first. Finally, she decided to just be honest. "I live in Washington, yes, but what my résumé doesn't include is that I grew up in Dayton. And in Dayton's foster care system. When I decided on a major in college, social work seemed the perfect fit. I wanted to work in a system that, while not perfect, can only become better and stronger with people who care to make it so for the children and families in it. And I want to work in the very system that saved me from an unstable home with my mother, and—for good and bad—raised me."

A heartbeat of silence pulsed down the connection. "I understand." And for the first time, a little bit of warmth replaced the cool politeness in the other woman's voice. "I look forward to speaking with you again on Thursday. Have a good day."

"You, too. And thank you again."

Tennyson ended the call, staring out the wall of windows opposite her. Her heart continued to thud against her rib cage, but a smile slowly curved her mouth.

She was doing it. Changing her life. Potentially half a country away from Dom. If things went well with the telephone interview, then the next step might be a final, face-to-face meeting in Dayton.

If that happened, she would have no choice but to tell Dom the truth.

She closed her eyes.

Shit just got real.

Chapter Eight

Dom entered the ballroom of The Westin Bellevue Hotel where the black-tie fundraising gala was in full swing. In spite of his pretty boy, party animal image portrayed by the press, he didn't really care for these social events. Unless his presence was required by the team or business arrangements, he avoided them like the plague. The only person who seemed to detest them more was Ronin. Unfortunately, black tie didn't permit ripped jeans, T-shirts, and battered worker boots, which was the receiver's usual outfit of choice.

Yet, here Dom stood, tuxedo-ed out on a Monday night, in an elegant ballroom full of men and women dressed to the nines, instead of sitting on his couch, catching ESPN highlights and the newest episode of *The Coroner: I Speak for the Dead*. And all for Zeph's Jaybird Foundation, named for his grandmother, Josephine Black. For the nonprofit organization that provided support and assistance to inner-city and underprivileged kids across the nation through football, Dom would gladly throw on a monkey suit and back any event with both his presence and money. Zeph had just hosted their annual football camp in June, and Dom had volunteered there as well. It was a great cause, and he admired his friend for his devotion.

Moving farther into the room, he was stopped every couple of feet by people wanting to shake his hand or ask about the Warriors' chances for the post season. Post season. Hell, it was only October. They had four more months of ball to go before then. It didn't escape his notice that no one mentioned the previous day's loss to Buffalo. It'd been a heartbreaker that had gone to overtime, but in the end, they hadn't managed to pull it out. Any more losses like that, and he could also lose his starting position. And then his contract. His focus had to be on the next game, the next team, not one so far in the future. But he didn't voice any of this. Instead he pumped hands, accepted slaps to his back, and donned his public demeanor—big, friendly smile; charming manner; and clean language. Only his close friends understood that while the persona was a part of him, it wasn't all of him. With them, he could be brooding, rude, and have a gutter mouth. With them, he could show a little of his fear and worry about not carrying his team to a successful, winning season.

Speaking of his friends, he scanned the crowded space. Being six-foot-five sometimes had its advantages. But not in a room full of football players who stood just as tall, if not taller. He couldn't find Zeph, Ronin, or...Tennyson.

A huge fist squeezed his gut. She was supposed to be here tonight, and it would be the first time they'd seen each other since last Tuesday. The last six days were the longest they'd been apart since they'd first met, including when he'd moved out of their foster home and attended college.

This stretch of time had been—empty. Though he'd filled every moment with football as he prepared for the upcoming game—practice, studying, watching film—there'd still been something missing. Tennyson. Her presence, her laughter, her snarky comments, her friendship.

A kiss had caused the rip. Just proved he'd been right in stopping it before they could go further. Correction, before he took it further. Sex wasn't worth the damage it could wreak on their relationship. If a kiss had resulted in this cold warfare, what would've happened if he'd slid that robe off her and buried his cock inside her like he'd wanted to in that moment? Between his lack of desire for a relationship while his career was peaking and her desire for a commitment he wasn't able to give, he could lose her. Permanently. And he wasn't willing to risk that. Couldn't allow it to happen. He would no longer be fighting to keep her as his PA but for her to remain in his life.

And at this moment, with his future as starting quarterback uncertain and a couple of losses already staining their record, his focus had to be on his career, the game. He had to avoid distractions and be in control on and *off* the field.

The No Friends with Benefits pact the rest of his group had made after the train wreck that was Renee and Jason made more sense now than ever before.

"Well, it's about time you showed up, baby boy," a voice carrying a distinct Louisiana flavor said from behind him. "I thought I was gonna have to hunt you down with a switch."

Grinning, Dom turned around, arms outstretched. He gathered the older woman in his arms and held her in a tight but gentle embrace. Josephine Black might be diminutive in stature, but she was a giant in personality. When he'd first heard Zeph mention his grandmother, Dom had pictured a tall, wide-shouldered, masculine woman who would have no trouble ruling over her grandson and granddaughter, Zeph's younger sister. Reality had been a bit different. Just an inch or two over five feet, Josephine Black, with Zeph's same light brown skin and hazel eyes, was a lovely, almost elfin woman in appearance. Some might mistake her for meek…until she opened her mouth. Her deep voice boomed several sizes bigger than her size, and she was as subtle as a hammer to the balls.

And Dom adored the hell out of her.

Not just because she'd adopted him and Ronin like two of her own, but also because if his own grandmother hadn't died before he was born, he imagined she would've been like Josephine. Loving, Wonder Woman strong, and with a low tolerance for bullshit.

"Sorry, Miss Josephine. I lost track of time after practice. But you knew I was coming if only to see you." He brushed a kiss over her cheek, inhaling the scent of Chanel No. 5. "And you're looking gorgeous tonight." Not a lie. In a black, long-sleeved gown that swept her slim figure and glided over her feet, she was the image of mature sophistication and beauty.

"Oh please. That charm isn't going to work on me like one of your women." She waved off the compliment, though her eyes sparkled with amusement and pleasure. "Speaking of women..." She arched a thin eyebrow. "You usually have one hanging off your arm or trying to get down your pants." She clucked her tongue. "Just no shame. In my day, we at least tried to add a little mystery about whether or not we'd eventually give in. Now they're just handing it away like there's a fire sale on kitty cat."

Dom choked on a bark of laughter. Jesus Christ. The woman had no filter.

"I just decided to go solo tonight, Miss Josephine." Slipping an arm around her shoulders, he plucked a glass of champagne from a passing server's tray. He loved this woman to pieces, but he was going to need this alcohol. "So you've met Sophia. You like her?"

"Of course," she said, nabbing the glass of wine from his hand and taking a delicate sip. "She's perfect for Boo."

"Boo" being Zephirin. Dom swallowed a snicker at

the childhood nickname. Instead he chided, "I thought you couldn't drink with the blood-pressure medicine Zeph said your doctor put you on."

"Stay outta grown folks' business, baby boy," she drawled with another sip from the glass. "Now, since you want to do so much talking, tell me who's that with Tennyson. Nobody told me she was seeing someone new."

Shock ricocheted through him. Immediately, he scanned the room, searching for a familiar head full of tousled, dark curls. She hadn't mentioned bringing a date even before this last week of non-communication. Who was it? He frowned, still surveying the ballroom. Not another man she'd found on that dating site...

"*Ohhh*, you didn't know." Josephine chuckled. "Well, good for her."

Jerking his attention back to Zeph's grandmother, he asked, "Excuse me?"

She patted his arm. "Such manners. My boy picked his friends so well. But let me put it to you bluntly. I'm glad she's finding her some arm candy. She can't wait on you to finally open up those pretty blue eyes of yours and see what's been under your nose all this time." She couldn't possibly mean... Wait. Did she know about the kiss...? A second later, relief swept through him. No, she couldn't possibly. He hadn't told anyone, and he was pretty damn sure Tennyson hadn't. "Miss Josephine, Tenny and I are—"

"Just friends," she finished the sentence, shaking her head. "I know, I know. Still, you have a beautiful woman right in front of you, and blind fool that you are, you just ignore her for those silly nitwits who just want you for what you have and what you do. And they're all so damn skinny to boot." She tsked. "Baby boy, the only thing that wants bones is a dog—and it buries those."

Caught between laughter and a groan, Dom tilted his

head back on his shoulders. How had this conversation taken such an awkward turn?

"There's Tennyson," Josephine announced.

Lifting his head, he glanced in the direction she pointed her glass.

And froze.

Even his breath stalled in his lungs. He couldn't move. Couldn't do anything. But stare. And feel. God, did he feel. Lust crackled like a live wire, prickling his skin, sizzling down to his cock. His flesh throbbed even as his chest tightened to the point of caving with the slightest pressure.

She was fucking beautiful.

Like living flame in a floor-length gown the color of fire. Liquid fire since the material poured over her gorgeous body like a jealous lover until it flared mid-thigh, reminding him of that chick from the *Hunger Games* movie Tennyson had made him watch. The sexy, plunging V of the dress showcased the perfection of her breasts while still remaining elegant and sophisticated. And those almost black spirals that had been wrapped around his fist a week ago tumbled around her face and brushed her shoulders in wild abandon.

Jesus, his palms and fingers itched to touch—her hair, her golden skin, her dangerous curves...the invitation of that lush mouth.

Every recrimination and resolution he'd made over the week and just minutes ago about never crossing that friendship line again vaporized under the heat of painful need. All he could think about was tasting those lips. Holding the weight of her breasts in his hands. Having what was between those gorgeous thighs welcome his aching erection.

Yeah, he wanted between those legs like he wanted a ring and trophy.

In this instant? Fucking more.

"Uh-huh," Josephine drawled, her voice reaching him

through a thick fog of arousal. "Just friends." With a chuckle, she walked off, disappearing into the crowd.

He spared her a glance, but immediately, his attention snapped back to Tennyson. Unable not to stare. To covet. His goddamn best friend.

The thought slammed into him like a linebacker. Rocking him back on his heels.

He needed to head in the opposite direction from her. Away from temptation until he got ahold of this unprecedented, crazy-as-all-hell reaction to her. He shifted backward, but then she looked up. Met his gaze.

And all his best intentions went up in smoke.

. . .

Oh, she'd been doing so well.

Tennyson hadn't looked for Dom in the crowd once. Okay, maybe *once*. But that'd been when she'd first arrived at the gala, and she'd skimmed the room for everyone she knew. Therefore, technically, that didn't count. Or so she kept telling herself.

Still, until this moment, she'd been enjoying the night with Michael Ramsey, aka MikeInShiningArmor. Tall, handsome, with pretty green eyes, and boy, could he fill out a tux. So far, their conversation had been light, fun, and though he had a dog, he'd only mentioned the pet once. Not to mention he hadn't batted an eyelash when she'd informed him who he would be meeting tonight. Unlike Adam, he'd been impressed but not awestruck. Another point in Michael's favor. The only mark against him was his career—an intern in his second year of residency at Northwest Hospital and Medical Center. If this was to go further, visiting him at work would be an impossibility. No way would she ever willingly set foot in a hospital. She shuddered at the thought.

Still, she was enjoying herself. And if there wasn't this all-consuming need to skip out of the gala and rip his clothes off, well, sometimes passion evolved later. A sense of humor, having things in common, great conversation—those were equally important.

And why was she trying to convince herself how great a potential catch Michael was?

Oh right. Because her friend—and the man who did ignite that all-consuming need—stood across the room, staring at her with a hooded gaze that sent a low, insistent throbbing between her legs. She clenched her thighs to alleviate the ache, but it only increased the sweet pain. Thank goodness for the lining in her dress. Or else her nipples would be saluting God and country.

Damn, no man had the right to be so…virile. It was like he wore his sexuality as easily and comfortably as the tuxedo tailored to his body.

She braced herself as he strode forward in that sensual stalk that was fluid and wicked. Dom was a thing of beauty on the football field, and off it? That same athleticism, confidence, and grace imbued everything he did, how he moved, walked. A woman could get hot just from watching those wide shoulders and strong thighs…

Jesus. She turned away and smiled up at her date. *Get your shit together, girlfriend*. She had a perfectly nice, well-mannered, *available* man in front of her whose eyes had lit up with pleasure and admiration when he'd first seen her. He saw her as a woman, and from the way his gaze kept dipping to her mouth, actually *wanted* to kiss her.

And if this date should turn into another and another, she might actually be a priority in his life. He might put her first—a position she'd never been for anyone. With her mother, her desperate and deranged need for attention had come before Tenny and her health. With the foster parents, their own children or desire for the checks came first. And as much as Dom cared for her, football would always be his love, his number one.

She longed for someone to place her above everything, just as she would do for them. And who knew? Maybe Michael could be that man. One thing was for certain. Dom never could be.

That alone made Michael better for her—and her self-esteem—than Dom.

A large hand settled on her lower back, and damn, the heat from it slid under her dress to warm her skin, her freaking blood. She didn't need to glance over her shoulder to see who was attached to that palm. Only one stirred this reaction in her. Damn it.

"Hello, Tennyson," Dom greeted her. "You look beautiful tonight." He brushed his lips over her cheek, and she prayed he or Michael didn't notice the shiver that rippled through her.

Stepping closer to Michael, she forced a smile that felt stiff and awkward. God, this...rift between them hurt. "Thanks, Dom." Waving a hand at her date, she said, "I'd like you to meet Michael Ramsey. Michael, this is my friend and employer, Dominic Anderson."

"One of the best quarterbacks in the game." Michael grinned and extended his hand toward Dom. "It's a pleasure to meet you."

"Same here," Dom said, accepting his hand for a quick shake. "Sooo... How did you two meet?"

"None of your business," she interjected as Michael opened his mouth to reply. Surprise crossed his face, and she smiled, even though behind her lips she ground her teeth together so hard, her molars ached in protest. "A girl's gotta have some secrets."

"Hey!" Ronin suddenly appeared, slapping Dom on

the shoulder. Tennyson released a soft sigh, relieved at the reprieve. Relieved, that is, until the receiver turned a grin on Michael. "You must be the online date."

Tennyson groaned.

FML.

Ronin studied her, his dark eyebrow raised. "What? What'd I say? Was it a secret?"

"Not if you knew," Dom drawled. "And nice…suit."

Ronin peered down at his tuxedo jacket, dress shirt, faded jeans, and scuffed worker boots. "I thought so," he said with a shrug. "And I combed my beard," he added, stroking a hand down the thick, springy facial hair.

"Don't listen to him, Ronin," she said as the receiver leaned down and planted a smacking kiss on her cheek. "I think your toggery is…you."

"Toggery." Michael grinned, and she returned the wide smile. A man who knew his vocabulary. He was just looking better and better. "Great word. I think your clothes definitely make a statement," he complimented Ronin, stretching a hand toward him.

"Michael, this is Ronin Palamo, wide receiver for the Warriors. Ronin, Michael Ramsey, who, yes, I did meet online. Bigmouth," she grumbled.

Winking at her, Ronin gripped Michael's hand in a firm shake. "Nice to meet you. Mike, you must have balls of steel. You've met this one," the receiver jerked a thumb in Dom's direction, "and you haven't run toward the door yet. I like you."

"Oh for fuck's sake," Dom muttered, glaring at Ronin, who just grinned wider.

Michael chuckled, and Tennyson had to admire his composure and sense of humor in the face of the two giants across from him. "It's a real pleasure to meet you. I'm a huge fan of the team."

"He's obviously smart and has great taste, too." Ronin held out a fist toward Tennyson, and she had no choice but to bump it with her own. Though she'd rather place her fist somewhere else at the moment. "Keep this one."

"God, Ronin." A blush raced up her throat and poured into her face. The man had all the tact of a rampaging elephant. "Please ignore him," she implored Michael.

Her date shrugged, amusement gleaming in his gaze. "Kind of hard to do. I mean, he's like six-six… And he's wearing jeans with a tux jacket."

She laughed, really liking him. Maybe there could be something there…

Then she made the mistake of glancing at Dom.

Shadows deepened his blue eyes, and part of her longed to reach out to him, bug him until he spilled what was bothering him. As his friend, she had a good guess. She'd watched the game the night before, and the loss had hurt her, so she could only imagine how hard he was taking it. Probably shoveling every fault on his wide shoulders. A week ago, she wouldn't have had a problem comforting him. But that was a week ago. Before the kiss and this strain between them.

But now, she kept her hands to herself and didn't voice any questions or give him an opening. Because if he used that opportunity to apologize again for touching her, kissing her… If he once more expressed his regret at treating her like a desirable woman, she might lose her shit. And irrevocably damage their relationship.

"Tenny, can I speak with you for a minute?" he asked, the low, husky timbre of his voice stroking over her exposed skin.

Hell no. Her internal shout reverberated against her skull. No, she couldn't be alone with him feeling so vulnerable. God only knew what would tumble out of mouth.

"Sorry," she said with another of those fake smiles that seemed to be coming more and more often around him.

"Michael and I were just about to dance. I'll catch up with you later."

Grasping her date's hand, she led him toward the dance floor where other couples had already started to sway to the sultry tune played by the jazz band hired for the evening. Thank the Lord Michael didn't question her sudden need to bust a move.

Awesome. Now she was quoting old rap songs.

She definitely needed to get her stuff together if she were going to make it through the evening.

An hour later, she excused herself from Michael and headed toward the restroom. Sighing as she exited the ballroom, she surveyed the temporarily empty hallway. Before she could change her mind—or someone entered the corridor and caught her—she leaned against the wall and hurriedly removed her red heels. Clutching the shoes in one hand, she kneaded the toes and heels of her foot, not bothering to smother a moan. The heels were gorgeous but not meant to walk, dance, and stand around in for three hours. At least not by her. Women like Renee could with seemingly no issue, but they must have ankles of titanium. After massaging her other foot, she strode down the hall in search of the bathroom.

Just as she spotted the door to the women's restroom, a hand enveloped hers in an implacable grip and tugged her into a nearby room. If not for the telltale pebbling of her skin and the pleasure/pain tightening of her belly, she would've screamed bloody murder. But the only thing she feared as she scanned what appeared to be a storage room for extra tables and chairs was being alone with Dom.

Somehow, all her avoidance tactics this evening had been pointless.

Crossing her arms over her chest, she met her best friend's unwavering stare.

"Is all this really necessary?" she asked, feigning an indifference she'd never felt with this man.

"When every time I get within five feet of you, you find an excuse to run in the opposite direction? Yes."

"I haven't been running." She scowled, holding up the shoes she still held in her hand. "That would be impossible in these."

The corner of his mouth twitched in a faint half smile. But it disappeared, his solemn expression firmly in place. "You've been avoiding me."

"Correction. We've been avoiding each other for a week now. And Zeph's fundraiser isn't the best place to discuss it."

"Right," Dom drawled, sliding his hands into the front pockets of his pants. "Because of your date." He slowly shook his head from side to side. "What about the bros before hoes code?"

She glared at him, unfolding her arms to jab a finger at his chest, while ignoring the solid slab of muscle under her fingertip. "I don't know whether to be more offended over you calling Michael a ho, or me a bro." She scoffed. "Then again, yeah, I do. How do you know he's a ho? Isn't that a case of the pot calling the kettle black?"

A muscle ticked along his jaw, a sure sign of his rising temper. Well, good. "Why didn't you mention meeting up with another of those online men? I get we haven't spoken much in the last few days, but I think for something like this you could've made an exception."

She widened her eyes in exaggerated innocence. "Gee, let's see. Maybe because the last time you found out about one of my 'online men,' you crashed my date like a lunatic and made him think I was a drunk stripper." She glared at him. "And like I said earlier, it's none of your business. Now do you want to talk about why you snatched me in here? I have a date to return to."

His eyes narrowed on her, and instead of exasperation and annoyance, arousal coursed through her. That look spelled trouble. And the last time he'd pinned her with that particular stare, his tongue had ended up in her mouth.

And I don't want that.

Yes, you do.

Great. Her own brain was arguing with itself. She had to get out of this room and away from Dom, quick.

"At least you met him at a public event," he said.

She rolled her eyes, throwing her hands up. "Okay, so I guess we're *not* going to discuss why I'm in this room." Or the elephant in it, either.

"What do you know about him? Other than the fact that he obviously spends a lot of time on his hair," he mocked.

What the hell did that mean? So what if Michael gave attention to the short, blond strands and made sure they were groomed and styled. Unlike *some* people who thought running their fingers through their hair equated to brushing it.

"He's nice, respectful, has a sense of humor, handsome…" Ignoring his snort, she continued. "He volunteers at the homeless shelter, is educated, intelligent, a doctor—"

"A doctor?" he repeated, skepticism and an undercurrent of anger threading through the words. Whenever anything even remotely related to her past and phobia came up, that underlining fury was always present in Dom. "Does he know you'll never meet him at his job to have lunch with him?"

"Well, you know what? The topic of my Munchausen mother and resulting aversion to hospitals didn't have a chance to come up between 'It's nice to meet you,' and 'Are you down to fuck?'" she snapped along with her temper.

The same surprise that blanked his expression whipped

through her. Sex hadn't even been mentioned, much less discussed. So why she'd thrown that out there like a gauntlet, she had no idea. Dom just pissed her off that much. And maybe a tiny, vindictive part of her wanted to let him know that a man found her sexy. Unlike him.

The shock dissipated from Dom's face, leaving behind a frown so fierce, she would've backpedaled a step if she wasn't already pressed against the closed door. Not out of fear—she could never be afraid of him—but wariness of her own reaction. Of the prickles of excitement tinged with nerves that tickled her skin, under her arms, and her stomach.

"Tell me you don't actually plan on having sex with that guy," Dom growled, his hands sliding out of his pockets as he shifted closer.

Her breath snagged in her throat. "So what if I am? I believe this, too, falls under the heading of None of Your Business."

"Tennyson..."

But the little devil on her shoulder had beaten up the angel on the opposite one. And that imp had taken over and didn't allow Dom to finish. "Since he's a doctor, I bet he's great with his hands. Knows all the spots on the female body, being an expert in anatomy." She hummed in pleasure, even as she questioned the wisdom of pushing Dom. "And I've been checking out his hands and feet all night. They're *huge*. And you know what they say about big feet—"

One second she breathed slightly dusty storage-room air, and in the next, she inhaled hot, pissed-off male. Long-fingered, large hands used to palming footballs bracketed her head. A hard, giant body loomed over her, blocking out the scenery of stacked chairs and collapsed round tables. And the most beautiful face in the world bent over hers, breath tinted with the sweet, tart flavor of champagne grazing her lips. Hooded blue eyes stared down at her, and she shivered at the intensity she could almost feel on her skin.

If she were smart, she would shut it. Two hundred and twenty-five pounds of quarterback on the edge had her caged in. Yeah, if she had the brains God gave a gnat, she'd keep quiet…

"I bet he can go *all* night," she whispered.

His mouth crashed down on hers, silencing her with a thrust of his tongue between her lips. She wasn't surprised; she'd understood what she'd been doing. Had understood what goading him would result in. *This*. So when he angled his head and stroked deeper, she opened wider, giving him the *more* he demanded. His tongue tangled with hers, dueling, claiming. His strong teeth tugged at her bottom lip, sucking on it, before returning to her mouth. With a low moan, she offered herself up to him, letting him have it all. Have her. Because, God, she'd waited so long, dreamed so long, for this moment. And damn if she wouldn't wring it out for all its worth before it ended.

He abandoned her mouth, and when she emitted a soft sound of protest, he pressed a brief, firm kiss to her lips, then trailed them down her chin and jaw to her neck. As his mouth opened over her skin, his tongue dancing over her wildly beating pulse, the disappointed whimper turned into a pleading cry.

Desperation kept her hands pressed to the door behind her, fingers curled. The need to touch him raced through her like forest fire, but she resisted the urge, afraid one caress would yank him out of whatever lust-infused trance he'd fallen into. She wasn't anywhere near ready to spy the regret and sadness that had twisted his face a week ago after kissing her. She'd do whatever was necessary to stave that off. Even if for just a little while longer.

Her refusal to use her hands didn't stop her from arching into the sensual glide of his lips over her collarbone down to her chest. He blazed a trail of pure sensation over her flesh, licking the inner curves of her breasts revealed by the deep neckline of her dress. His teeth grazed, his tongue soothed. And all the while, her nails bit into her palms as the words, *please don't stop, please don't stop*, chanted in her head.

With a swift jerk, he dragged the dress's wide shoulder strap down her arm, leaving it above her elbow. Another tug, and the bodice covering her breast bared her red lace bra.

"God*damn*," he swore, voice rough, a little ragged. Brutal satisfaction tore through her. He sounded two seconds from losing control because of *her*. "You shouldn't be this fucking sexy," he rasped. "I shouldn't…"

Whatever he'd been about to utter was lost as he flicked her nipple with the tip of his tongue through the almost sheer material. She shuddered, pleasure ripping down her and heading straight for her sex. She loosed a small whimper at the ache there, shifting restlessly. He gave her another lick, this one slower, more indulgent.

"Oh Christ," she whispered, her voice cracking. Surrendering to the roaring need to touch, she burrowed her fingers in his hair, gripping the strands much like he'd done to her during their ill-fated kiss. "Suck it, Dom. Please, don't tease me." She'd waited so long, she couldn't bear his coy, playful caresses.

Surprise flashed through the hunger in his eyes, and something darker, more wicked, entered the blue depths. Maybe a warning of being careful of what she asked for. Not breaking their visual connection, he pushed aside the lace of her bra, lowered his head to her flesh again, and slowly, so fucking slowly, drew the rigid tip between his lips. Then sucked.

She thumped the back of her head against the door, her lips parting on a silent cry as his tongue swirled around her nipple, tugging, damn feasting. She arched so hard into him, her back nearly bowed.

Needing more, she released her hold on him to push the other strap down, including the bra's. Hell, she'd been fantasizing about this for years, never believing it would come true. Now that it had, she didn't have time to be shy. Not when arousal had her in its relentless, consuming grip.

He switched breasts, his fingers and cool air replacing his mouth. While he tweaked and pinched her damp nipple, his lips closed over the neglected one, giving it the same attention as its twin. God, every lap, every sweep and thrust of his tongue had her closing in on the blurry edges of orgasm. Just from him sucking her breasts. Shit, she'd thought that was a myth. But now, now he'd not only made her a believer but a fervent devotee.

As if a marionette string ran from her nipples to her clit, each pull and strong suck had her hips jerking, her thighs twitching. Anything to alleviate the pressure building and building between her legs. Jesus, she needed him to touch her. Stroke. Lick. Damn it, she just needed him.

As if reading her mind, he dropped a hand to her waist and fisted the material over her hip, bunching it so the hem of her dress rode higher and higher. Baring her legs. Allowing the cool, stale air in the storage room to graze her flesh. But she wanted more than recycled air brushing the insides of her thighs. Impatient, she grabbed the other side of the gown and dragged it up.

Straightening, he curved his fingers under her thigh and hooked her knee over his hip, opening her wide. She shuddered, more aware than ever of the damp silk covering her sex. It wouldn't take much to set her off. She was so aroused, so turned on, that one caress, one slide of his finger through her folds, and she would explode. Another shiver rippled through her. Because she craved that. So bad.

Lowering his head, he clamped his teeth on the sensitive

tendon running the length of her neck. And his fingers—*oh Jesus, his fingers*—they skimmed over her stomach, glided over her hip, and slid beneath her panties. And thrust inside her.

The scream clawed up her throat, pushed its way into her mouth. No teasing preamble, no preparatory caresses. Just that firm, hard stroke that set her on fire…and set her off. She detonated around his finger, felt her flesh grasping at him as she tumbled helplessly into ecstasy.

He rode her through it, his knuckles bumping her clit, dragging out the pleasure until she sank her teeth into her bottom lip and could do nothing but whimper.

Soon, too damn soon, the storm eased. Her head cleared of the red-tinged passion-filled haze, and the world expanded to include the low click and whir of the air conditioning, her harsh breaths echoing in her head, and the pressure of his thick finger still wedged inside her.

Lifting his head from the crook of her neck, Dom met her undoubtedly wide gaze. What in the *hell* had just happened? The same shock darkened his eyes, and she could do nothing but stare mutely up at him. Slowly, he eased his finger from her body, and unbidden, she gasped, her core clutched at him, as if resenting his abandonment. His full lips firmed, and a muscle ticked along his jaw.

Arousal flagged his cheekbones, and one glance down affirmed the presence and size of an erection that left her mouth dry. She'd just exploded in the most delicious, bone-melting orgasm she'd ever experienced—even previous releases delivered courtesy of her own hand—and already need slid through her veins, prepping her for round two.

But she didn't need to study his expression to know there wouldn't be another go. Already, tension invaded his big body, and his arms lowered to his side, his fingers curled into fists. He didn't reach for her, or for his cock that pressed against his pants leg. No, he had no intention of finishing what they'd started. Or what she'd goaded him into.

Anger sizzled under her skin. Humiliation and anguish settled in her chest like a huge boulder, bearing down, squeezing. Hell no, she refused to look into his face. Because last time, the remorse and pity had stabbed her in the heart. This time, it would obliterate the stupid, treacherous organ.

In seconds, she jerked her dress down and tugged the dress straps back into place. Whipping around, she snatched up her shoes, yanked open the door and tripped out in the hallway. She didn't even glance back when Dom called her name. Cutting a direct path to the bathroom, she didn't acknowledge him or the harsh curse he uttered as he followed her. She shoved into the bathroom and hurriedly twisted the lock in case he even thought about barging in to explain. To talk.

To apologize.

To explain why it shouldn't—and couldn't—happen again.

Sinking onto the floral-upholstered couch, she avoided the mirror hanging on the wall opposite her. She had an idea of what she looked like. Smeared lipstick over a kiss-swollen mouth. Rumpled dress. Flushed face. In other words, like a woman who'd just been sexed and discarded.

And she had herself to blame.

Covering her face with her hands, she swallowed the sob that welled up in her throat. And yet, she wasn't completely successful because the tail of it echoed in the room.

Not again. She wouldn't permit herself to be a fool again.

Chapter Nine

Dom slammed his gloved hands into the black punching bag, sending it swinging on its chain. He skipped back as it swayed toward him, and then he bobbed and weaved, throwing another fist. The impact sent a vibration singing up his arm and into his shoulder. Ordinarily, his workout didn't include the punching bag, but today, when he needed to excise the confusion and frustration that had kept him awake all night, lifting weights wouldn't cut it.

An image of Tennyson last night in that temptation of a dress floated in front of him. Right on its heels, another vision of her solidified. Her, the same dress rucked up around her thighs; lips, plump from his mouth, parted; pretty brown eyes glazed with passion. Grinding his teeth together, he delivered another blow to the bag.

Her voice, whispering, demanding. *Suck it, Dom. Please, don't tease me.* Another punishing ram of his fist. And another. And another.

By the time he finished twenty minutes later, sweat rolled off his body like little runoff streams, his shoulders and arms were tight…and he still hadn't beaten away the memories.

Especially the last one. When she'd bolted from him like he'd sprouted razor-sharp teeth and claws.

Jesus Christ. Disgusted, he unlaced his gloves and wrenched them off, throwing them on the floor of his home gym. He shouldn't have cornered her, should've left well enough alone.

When he'd scoped out the storage room at the gala earlier, catching her and starting the talk they should've had days ago had been his only intention. A conversation about them, their friendship, and clearing the air so they could move on from this stumbling block.

He definitely hadn't intended to discuss her online date, *Michael*. Or grow angry over her contemplating out loud how good sex would be with the guy.

Or shove his hand under her skirt and finger-fuck her pussy.

"Shit." His whisper reverberated off the stark white walls and mirrors in the room. He'd messed up. Badly. He'd glimpsed her face before she'd escaped the storage room. Had spotted the embarrassment and hurt in those expressive chocolate eyes. Had caught the tremble of her soft mouth.

The person in this world he loved most, and he'd caused her pain because he'd allowed his dick to override his brain.

Now how did he fix it? Fix *them*? Because losing her wasn't an option. Yet, the last two times they'd been together, he'd committed the very sin capable of destroying their friendship.

And now that he intimately knew how slick and tight she was, how wet she got? The hunger that should've been extinguished by the danger of causing harm to their relationship only burned hotter and brighter with the knowledge. He couldn't scrub it from his mind. Couldn't erase the sound of her cries from his brain. Couldn't forget how she'd tasted—both her mouth and her breasts. Couldn't wipe out how she'd come apart with just one thrust of his fingers.

Women sought him out to get in his bed for any number of reasons. A chance at a relationship. Fifteen minutes of fame. Money they hoped to get out of him. Hell, a notch on their own belt. And they pulled out all the sexual acrobatics and stunts to make themselves memorable. But none of their wild positions or porn star–worthy performances had made him as hard, as close to losing it as Tennyson shuddering in his arms, features taut with passion, her sex sucking him deep.

Maybe if he could find a way to demolish those memories, he could find the resolve and strength not to drive over to her apartment and finish what he started the night before.

Because even knowing how sex would possibly fuck up their relationship, *damn*, he wanted to finish.

Stripping his shirt off, he strode toward the bathroom off the gym. Minutes later, he stepped under the pounding spray of the shower water. As he scrubbed away the sweat from his workout, he wished he could as easily wash away this almost unfathomable need for his best friend.

With a low curse, he twisted the knobs and stepped out of the glass-enclosed space that was big enough to fit about five people. He toweled off, dragged on a clean pair of black sweatpants, and padded barefoot up the stairs. His schedule was open until a ten o'clock meeting with his agent tomorrow morning. Sunday was a bye week, so he had today and Wednesday off, and then the weekend. Four free days to relax, recuperate, and drive himself nuts thinking about…

"Tenny." He blinked, but nope, she still stood there in his foyer as if his thoughts had conjured her. Lust, worry, relief, unease—they rushed through him like an all-out blitz. He braced under the impact.

"Hey." She faced him, and if not for her white-knuckled

grasp on her messenger bag strap and subtle clenching of her jaw, he would've thought her completely composed. Unaffected. But after so many years of friendship, he knew her tells. "I thought you were downstairs, so I was just grabbing a couple of things I left last week..." She patted the front of her bag.

"You mean, you intended to sneak in and out of here before I came upstairs," he translated, voice flat.

Irritation flashed across her face, and her shoulders drew back. The move thrust her breasts forward, and he couldn't help noticing how her long-sleeved shirt molded over them. Couldn't help wondering what color bra she wore. Since the night she'd shown up at his house three sheets to the wind, he'd formed a small obsession with her bras and underwear. Black lace. Red lace. Or maybe it was how the sexy lingerie appeared against her soft, golden skin that he'd become obsessed with.

He yanked his hungry gaze away from her body and up to her face. And caught her eyes fixed on his bare chest. Hot arousal mixed with satisfaction swirled in his gut and lower. If she didn't stop staring at him as if picturing herself tracing every line of his tattoos with her tongue, then his sweatpants would do a piss-pot poor job of concealing the effect of her attention. Already his cock pulsed, hardening. In another few seconds, no way could she miss what she was doing to him.

"Tenny?" he murmured.

"I wasn't sneaking," she said, a slight rasp roughening the denial. She scowled. "You were downstairs working out, and I didn't want to disturb you."

He slowly shook his head. "You were always a shit liar."

Her eyes narrowed, her chin notching up in a defiant gesture that had his fingers curling into his palms in a desperate attempt to keep his hands off her. "You would be surprised at how good I am at hiding things."

He arched an eyebrow. "Meaning?"

"Nothing," she said.

A sense of disquiet wormed its way through him. Had she been keeping something from him? She'd been the one reliable, predictable constant in his life. Her and football. But lately, he sometimes felt like he didn't know her as well as he thought.

"Where you off to? About to meet up with Michael?" He tried to keep the dark slick of feeling that smacked too damn close to jealousy for his comfort out of his voice. *Tried* to.

Her mouth tightened, and he prepared himself for the *none of your business* that was all up in her expression. Instead, after a moment, she shook her head. "No. We agreed last night to just remain friends." She sighed. Glancing away from him, she thrust her fingers through her hair, and the phantom caress of those curls over his palms whispered over his closed fists. "Listen, Dom…"

"I'm not sorry," he interrupted, the words propelling from him. She blinked at him, and he commiserated with her surprise. He hadn't meant to utter those words. But he wasn't taking them back either.

He couldn't.

Because he meant them.

"I didn't feel that way about twenty minutes ago," he admitted to her and himself. "I was just downstairs beating the hell out of a punching bag because I'd again crossed a line with you I shouldn't have. But I was also trying to forget how good you tasted. How sweet you moan when you come. How tight you squeezed my fingers…how wet you got them." Her soft gasp of air reached him across the foyer. Her eyes widened, and the pulse at the base of her throat fluttered like a trapped butterfly's wings. "Yeah," he said, nodding. "Until I walked up here and saw you, I'd convinced myself I could stop all this in its tracks. That I needed to. But fuck," he whispered. "I can't pretend to be noble when all I'm thinking about is getting my mouth on you. Getting yours on me. Yeah, I've been having a real hard time not imagining you on your knees in front of me putting that pretty mouth to work."

The shock in her eyes melted away to a heat that burned through his veins, lighting him up like a stadium on *Monday Night Football*. Still, he forced himself to stand there, not rush her like he had the previous two times they'd kissed.

This time, he needed her to come to him. Show him that she craved this like he did. Whatever "this" was. His view of relationships hadn't changed, and neither had his priorities when it came to his career. The two didn't mix. But in this instant, all he cared about was burying himself inside her.

"Kiss me," he ordered. Or maybe begged.

• • •

Disbelief rooted Tennyson to the floor, paralyzing her.

"Kiss me." The sultry sexuality in Dom's invitation wrapped around her, stroking over her suddenly sensitive skin. Every nerve ending had sprung to life and stood at attention, turning her into a living divining rod for the arousal that simmered in his eyes. And tented the front of his sweatpants.

Jesus Christ.

The breath *whooshed* from her lungs. Riveted, she started at the outline of his cock. The material did nothing to hide the thick column or the wide head of his erection. And damn, it was both thick and wide. A tribal beat set up between her legs, and she just managed to swallow a moan.

I've been having a real hard time not imagining you on your knees in front of me putting that pretty mouth to work.

His rough, low words from only moments earlier reverberated in her head, filling her brain with the same visual. Her, sinking in front of him, hooking her fingers in the band of his pants, and drawing them down. Revealing that beautiful cock that could be hers. If she had the courage to claim it.

Yanking her gaze up his body, she met his unwavering scrutiny. There was a dare in those blue eyes. As well as a need that miraculously mirrored the desire twisting her inside out. But could she trust it? Would he turn away from her again, leaving her aching with unfulfilled passion and her heart hurting from his pious rejection?

Did she care?

She shivered. That was the real question. Did she risk all that to finally discover what being possessed, penetrated, and taken by Dom felt like? She'd dreamed of the moment when he would look at her not as his best friend, but as a desirable woman he wanted to fuck. He could shake his head in two seconds, realize what he was doing, and rescind that invitation. Then where would she be? The same place she'd been for a decade. Longing. Alone. The little "sister" she'd never asked to be.

She planned on leaving Seattle whether the job in Dayton came through or not. There were other employment opportunities, and her decision to move on from him, grab a life, and live it hadn't changed.

But she could either leave having grasped this opportunity to give herself to him and take him for herself…or she could leave a coward too scared to trade fantasy for reality.

Before the answer fully formed in her head, her feet moved across the foyer.

In seconds, rock-hard muscle met her hands. With a sigh she didn't bother to contain, she slid her palms over his chest, the heat that emanated from him warming them. God, the man was like a furnace—a furnace encased in taut, inked skin.

He didn't move under her exploration, and pleasure hummed through her at the open access he silently granted her. *Kiss me*, he'd said. And she complied. But when she parted her lips, it was to trace the tattoo of the broken pocket watch with her tongue on his lower stomach.

A hiss sounded above her seconds before two large hands burrowed through her hair, gripping the strands. "I fucking knew that's what you were thinking," he growled, pressing her closer to him.

The words didn't make sense to her, but then his earthy scent of cedar, rain, and fresh soap distracted her. As did the slight sting to her scalp from his tight hold on her hair. She returned the favor by raking her teeth over the roots of the olive tree that hugged his side and the branches that soared up his torso. A hoarse curse was her reward as well as the ridged muscles of his abdomen going concave under her mouth. And when she licked the spear and shield Warriors emblem covering his right pectoral, pausing to suck the flat, dark brown disc of his nipple, he yanked her head back, kissing her with a hunger that left her breathless.

His tongue thrust between her lips, and his unyielding grip on her head held her prisoner to the claim he staked on her mouth. Not that she was trying to escape. No, she clasped his wrists, rose on her toes, and opened wider for him. This time it was her issuing the invitation to take, conquer. To fuck.

Part of her couldn't believe she actually stood here with Dom, kissing him. And him returning the embrace as if she were the last meal he would receive for the next year. It almost seemed like a dream. One she didn't want to wake up from. A bolt of desperation blasted through the lust, and she released his wrists, running her palms up his shoulders, down his sides, and stroking up his back. As if she had to hurry and touch and caress before the opportunity was snatched from her. She had to soak it all in before she lost this chance…

"Slow down, sweetheart," he murmured against her lips. "We're not rushing this. Up."

He palmed the backs of her thighs and hoisted her in his arms even without her help. The show of strength shouldn't have had her head swimming, but damn if it didn't. She wasn't a lightweight, but he made her feel like one. Encircling his neck with her arms and his waist with her legs, she covered his mouth in another kiss. His hands shifted from her legs to her ass, and she squirmed against him. And her eyes nearly rolled in the back of her head as the movement rubbed her sex over his dick. Pleasure spread from between her legs, up her belly, and into her breasts, teasing her nipples into tight points. With a whimper, she flexed her hips again, and God, it was so *good*.

"Keep that up, and we're not going to make it to the bed," he warned, his fingers pressing harder into her behind. The firm grip on her flesh had her momentarily forgetting how much she had back there. She couldn't remember much past the increasing dampness in her panties as the head of his cock bumped her clit with each step he took.

Seconds later, he nudged the door to his master suite open and lowered her to the bedroom floor. And that quick, the modesty and embarrassment rushed in as if they'd just been waiting on the periphery to infiltrate and remind her she was about to get naked with Dom. And she didn't possess the slender, tall body of the kind of woman he usually took to bed. With normal men like Michael or Adam, she would've been fine, not self-conscious. But Dom was far from normal. He had the body of a god and was used to fucking goddesses. Not mortal women with breasts, asses, and a dimple here and there like her.

"Whatever you're thinking, stop it." His harsh demand whipped through the room. She lifted her head, not even aware she'd lowered it, and met his narrowed gaze. Though arousal gleamed there, so did anger. At her. "That's right, Tenny, lift your head. Look at me. Or better yet..." He enfolded her hand in his and, without offering her much choice, led her past the king-sized bed with its luxurious, dove gray comforter and black, leather headboard as well as the bank of floor-to-ceiling windows that looked over the fire pit and pool. He paused in front of a black leather ottoman and the large mirror that nearly covered the opposite wall. "Look at you."

"Dom," she whispered, shyness and mortification eddying inside her, threatening to swamp desire. She fixed her gaze on the low piece of furniture, unable to study their reflections. She shifted, trying to angle her body away from the mirror, but one big hand settled on her hip, holding her in place, and the other grasped her chin. The grip on her face was gentle but implacable, and he brooked no resistance as he turned her head until she had no choice but to look into the glass.

In spite of her embarrassment, a shiver rippled through her. He stood over a foot taller than her, so the top of her curls brushed his chin. With the wide span of his shoulders, the length of his arms, and the strength in his thighs, he damn near surrounded her. She appeared almost delicate compared to him. In bed, he would totally cover her, and the thought had air whistling from between her parted lips. Had flames licking at her skin and sizzling currents traveling back and forth between her nipples and sex.

"What was it you once said?" he said, pushing her hair from the side of her neck and lowering his head until his lips grazed her throat. "I don't want short women with ass for days who carry twenty extra pounds? Did I get that right?" When she didn't reply, he nipped the crook of her neck. She whimpered, her knees softening to the consistency of jelly. "Did I get that right?" he asked again. She nodded, momentarily muted. "Is that how you see yourself?"

He knew her better than anyone, so she didn't bother answering. And when he nuzzled her throat, and she saw as well as felt the flick of his tongue over her pulse, she couldn't have found her voice if it'd yelled Marco Polo.

"You say short; I say petite, graceful." His hand abandoned her hip and slid down and around, cupping her ass. She started, fire racing to her face at the possessive touch. "Shh," he soothed, his gaze locking with hers in the mirror. His fingers squeezed, molded her flesh, and she groaned, part mortified, part out of need. "Ass for days?" he quoted. "I say perfection. An ass that men fantasize about in bed… An ass they jack off to." The crude words should've turned her off. But yeah, all she could think about was Dom being one of those men. "And twenty extra pounds?"

In a lightning-fast movement, he tugged her arms in the air, whipped her shirt over her head, and tossed it to the floor. Stunned, she stood frozen in her lavender bra and jeans. She could only watch as his arms enfolded her and his hands cradled her breasts. The warmth of his palms, his fingers curving around her flesh, shattered the numbness. With a strangled cry, she arched into him, her arms raising and locking behind his neck. When her lashes fluttered, he rumbled a denial, the sound vibrating against her back.

"Look at yourself," he ordered. "You're not heavy, Tennyson. You're a woman. With a woman's curves." He squeezed her, and her nipples pressed against his palms. She bowed harder, craving more of that pressure. Needed him to alleviate the ache. Increase the ache. Hell, she didn't know. She just needed him to touch her.

"Please," she pleaded, entranced by the sight of his large hands on her. "Touch me."

"Here?" he murmured, his fingertips sweeping over her chest. "Here?" He teased a wide circle around each breast.

"Or...here?" Those wicked fingers captured her nipples, pinching them.

"Yes, damn it," she breathed, electricity arcing from the tips to her sex. She twisted in his embrace, and her breath snagged in her throat as she caught sight of herself. Undulating in his arms, her face flushed, eyes fevered, hair more wild than usual from his hands.

"Now you see it," he said into her ear. He rolled the peaks, alternating between soft sweeps and this-side-of-punishing tweaks. A cry slipped from her lips, and the pleasure coursed through her veins, melted her from the inside out. "That's you. Beautiful, sexy, uninhibited."

With a low snarl, he tumbled her to the ottoman. From one moment to the next, she went from standing to lying on the seat, her hips resting on the edge of the furniture. Kneeling in front of her, he snatched off her boots, then unbuttoned her jeans and yanked them down her legs. Her underwear immediately followed, leaving her naked except for her bra.

He cupped her knees and spread her wide, his gaze pinned on her bared flesh.

"Dom...*God*." The cry exploded from her and ricocheted around the room. Her fingers tangled in his hair, pulling, but his mouth stayed right where it was—on her sex. Jesus, she couldn't breathe, couldn't...think. Not with his tongue licking her clit, sucking it, grazing it with his teeth. He feasted on her like she was the sweetest, most delicious treat, and he'd been denied her for far too long. Long, wicked strokes parted her folds, lapping at her, swirling, and—if the low hum vibrating against her was any indication—savoring her.

She pushed her hips up, offering herself to him even as she yanked at his hair to pull him away. Mindless. Confused. Swamped in the craziest lust. He'd transformed her into this creature that clawed at his scalp and rode his mouth in sexual abandon.

And when he slipped two fingers inside her, she screamed her pleasure for God and country to hear. He shifted back to the top of her sex, his lips latching onto her clit again as he thrust up into her, his fingertip curling, stroking an area high and unknown until this moment. He massaged the spot, pulling and sucking on the too-sensitive bundle of nerves.

Relentless. He was relentless, and a part of her shrank from the cataclysm that reached for her, awaited her. But heat sizzled the soles of her feet, culminating and spinning deep inside her. With one last cry, she surrendered, toppling over the edge.

He continued to rub and lick, giving her every measure of the orgasm. Only when she shuddered, the electric waves receding, did he slip free and lift his head. His mouth glistened with the evidence of her arousal, making it appear lush, carnal. And as he slicked his tongue over his lips, she suddenly wanted to taste herself on that mouth.

Reaching for her hand, he helped her sit up and then slide off the ottoman. With careful but urgent hands, he guided her until she faced away from him, the edge of the furniture pressing into her belly. Those same hands removed her last remaining piece of clothing, then threaded through her hair. Her lashes fluttered closed at the caress that was both sensual and tender. Even as the embers of need stirred again, so did the trembling in her heart. And for the first time since she'd crossed that foyer to kiss him, doubt over her decision filtered through her. Would she be able to walk away after this, knowing it had never been just sex to her, as it was to him? Had she made the most colossal mistake of her life?

"You okay?" His chest aligned with her back, and, with a gentle tug on her hair, he brought her head to rest on his shoulder. He brushed a kiss over the bridge of her nose, the corner of her mouth, her jaw. "You still with me?"

God, he was so attuned to her. Fear that she would never feel this connection to another man speared her chest. But that fear wouldn't stop her from seizing this moment and hoarding it for the future when he was hundreds of miles away.

"Yes," she whispered, running her lips under his chin.

"Good. Because after tasting you..." He exhaled, his fingers tightening in her hair. "I want to be inside you."

He moved behind her, and a glance in the mirror revealed him shoving his sweatpants down below his hips and ass. Those embers flared to hot, dancing flames. The hard, firm muscles of his ass flexed as he gripped the base of his cock and stroked up...and up the length, his fist twisting when it covered the head. She swallowed, a deep ache yawning wide inside her along with a flurry of feminine anxiety. He was... impressive. Screw it. He was huge, and it would soon fill her. She craved it more than her next heartbeat, but...*God*.

"You still on the Pill?" he asked, the quiet question a soft breeze against her cheek. She nodded; he sometimes picked up her prescriptions from the drug store, but the inquiry still surprised her. "We need a condom?"

Her heart thudded against her chest, and her fingers curled into the cushion of the ottoman. "Do you use one with...?" She couldn't voice the rest of the sentence since just the thought of him with other women had knots twisting in her stomach.

"Always," he immediately replied.

The implication slowly sank in. With the...others he protected himself. But with her, he didn't have to. And except for her heart, she didn't have to with him.

"No. We don't need a condom," she breathed.

He stilled, then a shudder shook him, echoing through her. One of his hands cupped her hip, and the other smoothed up her spine and curled around the back of her neck. And pressed.

She obeyed the unspoken direction, lowering her upper body to the ottoman, her cheek and stomach pressed to the cushion, her arms stretching above her head and grasping a hold of the opposite edge. She waited, teetering on a precipice for him to fill her, brand her. And when his cock nudged her entrance, she couldn't contain a moan. Even knowing that taking him wouldn't be easy—not with his size and it having been at least two years since she'd last had sex—she wanted it. Craved it...craved him.

He pushed into her, and the burn, the stretch of his cock possessing her drove the breath from her lungs. Squeezing her eyes shut, she gritted her teeth against the fire-laced pressure. And yet, underneath prowled the knowledge that this was *Dom* slowly, steadily burying himself inside her. That reality reignited the fire that had dimmed with the startling claiming of her body. And when he finally stopped driving forward, when he stilled and only the thunder of their harsh breath reverberated in the room, she lifted her lashes and peeked at her and Dom in the mirror.

They could've been an erotic statuette in a museum— frozen in the very act of seeking carnal pleasure, his powerful, godlike body etched in stark relief, hips pressed to her ass, clutching her to him. Beautiful. Sexual. And perfect.

Gradually, as if each ticking second uncorked one of her senses, more sensations poured into her. The heady scent of their arousal, the sweat and musk that dampened their skin. The almost too-firm clench of his fingers into her hips. The bright, fevered stare that studied the place of their intimate connection. The faint flavor of his kiss still lingering on her tongue and lips. The discomfort between her legs ebbing and sliding into something darker, heated, and hungry.

As if he sensed her gaze on him, he met hers in the glass. His eyes had always been an impossible shade of blue, but aflame with lust, they burned even brighter, hotter. Lowering his chest to her back, he covered her, his arms extending along the length of hers, his fingers curling over hers. They stared, together, as his hips flexed and rolled, and he massaged her feminine walls with his cock. *Ohhhh God*. He touched places in her... Her lashes fluttered, falling...

"No, sweetheart," he whispered in her ear. "Open your eyes. Look at us. Look at me fucking you. Look at you taking me. I knew you could." Another roll of those hips. Another deep stroke that stoked the need in her higher until she could only whimper. "So sweet, baby. God*damn*, this pussy..."

He'd never spoken to her like this before—guttural, raw, dirty. And she *loved* it. She wanted to be his baby. His sweetheart. And if that didn't mean she'd taken a left at Lost Your Fucking Mind Avenue, she didn't know what did. But if he talked to her again in that graveled voice and did that *thing* again with his dick, she'd set up stakes and camp out there.

Trailing his lips down her spine, he grabbed her hips, hitched them higher, and drove into her. She hung on—to the ottoman, her senses, her sanity. With each plunge inside her, he shoved her closer and closer to the brink.

She greedily backed into each thrust. She chased release like an erotic game of hide-and-go-seek. Scrambled after it. Every dark grunt he emitted...every time she glimpsed the thick column of his cock glistening with her before he slammed inside her sex again...every slap of skin against skin... They all propelled her closer and closer to the crumbling edge that loomed so near but so damn far away...

"I'm not coming without you," he growled, curving a hand around the base of her neck and drawing her back and against his chest.

The fingers remained, circling her throat. He didn't exert pressure, but the weight of the caress, the possessive grip, it sizzled through her like a high-voltage current. And when he slipped the fingers of his other hand between her spread thighs and pressed her clit, the current exploded in a burst of light, heat, and fire.

She screamed, convulsed, and splintered, plunging into an orgasm that had her heart spasming in rapture and fear. Because even as she plummeted into the welcoming arms of darkness, and Dom stiffened behind her, his raw, hoarse curses blistering her ears, a part of her still-conscious mind registered that nothing would ever be the same between them.

Nothing.

Chapter Ten

Dom blinked, for a moment disoriented. The lavender, gray, and pearlescent sky outside his bedroom window telegraphed it had to be about six o'clock. But he never slept during the day or early evening. Not even for a nap. His days off were often packed with the appointments he couldn't make during the week because of his practice and travel schedule, so rest was usually a pipe dream.

But it was Tuesday, dusk, and he'd just woken up in his bed. Naked.

Naked.

As if the sight of his bare chest and dick kicked open the door to his memory, images flooded in, speeding through his brain like a subway train without brakes. Fucking Tennyson on the floor. Her riding him on the bed. Him with his face buried between her thighs.

He scrubbed a hand down his face, sighing. And waited for the remorse to sweep in, covering him in guilt and self-directed anger. But…nope. Nothing. Except for his hardening dick at the memories that continued to stream like the trailer of an X-rated movie.

Sighing, he sat up, shoving the bedcovers to the side. He didn't need to glance behind him to verify Tenny wasn't asleep, curled up in the tangled sheets. After being in each other's lives for so long, a connection had been forged. He could sense her presence, just as he was certain she could feel his. And his instincts informed him that she didn't linger in the bed or the bathroom. Considering the line they'd not just crossed but obliterated, he wouldn't be surprised if she'd left the house.

Shit. While he didn't regret the sex—sex, such an anemic word to describe what had transpired between them—unease crawled into his chest and squatted there. Absently, he rubbed the low-grade ache. Except for his explicit and yeah, admittedly dirty demands, they hadn't spoken for the hours they'd been wrapped around each other. They damn sure hadn't talked beforehand about how fucking would change their friendship. Or if they would even have one left to change.

They needed to have that conversation. Because even as his dick throbbed just with the thought of being wrapped in her tight sex, his heart pounded at the possibility of losing the one person who'd known him the longest. The person who'd been his family when he'd lost his to fate's fickle bitch ass. It'd been a while since the grief had clawed him bloody and loneliness had strangled him with its ever-tightening noose. But the pain and emptiness were still familiar. He could still taste their faint bitter flavor on the back of his tongue. Tennyson had eased their grip all those years ago, and no matter what, he couldn't sacrifice their relationship.

And then there was football. Once, he'd almost jeopardized his future for a woman, a relationship that hadn't been true or real. He'd allowed himself to get so wrapped up in her that it'd messed with his game, his friendships, and his heart. He couldn't permit himself to revert to that man again. Couldn't let that loss of control affect every aspect of his life. Especially his career. Not when so many people—including himself—depended on him showing up, focused, determined, and ready.

But he also wanted the soul-ripping pleasure he'd discovered in Tennyson's body. Fuck, riding her bare... It'd been a damn religious experience. The slick, snug, hot clasp of her pussy... He shuddered. Only with her did he dare screw without a condom; no other woman had earned that kind of trust. And he'd never imagined it could be so goddamn wonderful—perfect.

So no, he didn't want to give up either her friendship or the mind-altering sex. There had to be a way to keep one—at least for a little while—without irreparably harming the other. But in order to find that compromise, they first had to *talk*. Which meant he had to hunt her down.

Minutes later, he emerged from the shower, dragged on a fresh pair of sweatpants and a long-sleeved shirt. After stuffing his feet into a pair of sneakers, he jogged down the stairs. When he hit midpoint, the sweet, tangy aroma of frying onions and apple-smoke scent of grilling meat reached him. He descended the rest of the steps slower, though the delicious smells emanating from the rear of the house damn near had him salivating.

Only one person he knew could create culinary magic like that.

Tennyson hadn't left.

He headed toward the back of the house. Toward the kitchen.

• • •

Tennyson stood at the marble island, head bent, beating the cream cheese and spinach mixture in a bowl. Behind her, a pan of large mushroom caps was already cooking in the oven. After waking, she'd showered and cut a path directly for the kitchen, for her sanctuary. Dom might release his problems on a punching bag, but this was where she worked out her emotions, her issues, her frustrations. Which, she suspected, had been Dom's intention when he'd bought the house, remodeled the kitchen, and stocked it with top-of-the-line appliances and cookware.

She didn't turn around when he entered the room, but she didn't need to. She sensed him. Awareness sizzled and danced over her skin. Her shoulders tensed under her T-shirt, and she tightened her grip on the spoon in her hand.

Though she didn't remove her attention from the bowl, she heard him move farther into the room. His scent of freshly washed skin reached her before he did, and lured out images of the last few hours they'd just spent together. Of his hands slowly skimming her body as she undulated over him. She'd ridden him with no shame.

It was official.

She was a hussy.

"What're you cooking?" Dom asked the harmless question, but it did nothing to ease the tension zipping up and down her spine.

"Portobello mushrooms stuffed with spinach and steak," she said, never glancing up.

"What did that—whatever it is—do to you?" His hand closed over hers, stopping her very fervent stirring. Maintaining his hold on her, he inched closer and, lowering his head, nuzzled her curls.

She stilled, unable to release her stranglehold on the wooden utensil.

"Dom," she whispered.

"Yeah?"

"I'm cooking."

He snorted but edged away, granting her the space she needed.

She studied him, unease swirling in her chest. He didn't smile as he picked up one of the stools lining the breakfast bar on the other side of the room, lugged it over to the freestanding island, and sat, facing her.

"We need to talk," he announced.

Oh God.

The disquiet solidified into a leaden weight that sank to the bottom of her stomach. There shouldn't have been enough breath in her lungs to shudder out from between her lips. But she heard her own shaky gasp and prayed he hadn't.

"Now I know how men feel whenever women say that to them," she managed to mutter. The spoon clattered against the side of the bowl as her numb fingers released it.

"Sweetheart," he murmured, once more covering her hand with his. Slowly, she lifted her head and met his eyes for the first time since he'd entered the kitchen. "We need to have this conversation."

Sighing, she turned around to the stove. With deliberate movements, she tugged on her mitts and removed the pan from the oven and set it on the range. *It's okay. I can do this. I'm not going to break.* Even though her thudding heart begged to differ. *Jesus.* She briefly closed her eyes before taking off the mitts and pivoting to face him again.

"Fine." But before he could say anything, she lifted a hand in the age-old sign of "stop." He'd damn near destroyed her last time with the Friend Zone talk. Not again. She couldn't bear it again. "I already know what you're going to say. It was a mistake. We shouldn't have had sex. Bad for us, bad for our friendship—"

"Are you going to eventually breathe so I can speak?" he interrupted, voice calm, his eyebrow arched. "We're friends— best friends. And no matter what has happened, or happens from here on out, I need you to be my friend."

She nodded. "Me too," she agreed, unable to prevent the rasp roughening her voice. How she managed to speak past the thick lump in her throat was a miracle. Afraid her face would reveal the panic clawing at her, she dropped her gaze to the marble countertop.

"But I want to fuck you again. Even now, I want to strip those jeans off and burn them for getting in the way of me being inside you." He dropped his stare to her thighs, studying her as if the denim *offended* him.

The dread started to release its talons, and she blinked at him. Blinked again. "Okay," she breathed.

Wait. Where was this going? He didn't want to ruin their friendship...but he still wanted to fuck her. She was lost. Maybe... Fear, hope, excitement and dread coalesced in her belly, surging up until it filled her like a helium balloon, pressing against her rib cage. Maybe she should tell him about her feelings for him. Maybe, this time, with the intimacy they just shared, it would be different...

"Tenny," he said, then stopped, thrusting his fingers through his hair. "You know me better than anyone, so I won't lie. I don't want a relationship. Hell, you better than anyone know why. For me, football is my top priority, and I need it to be. I want it to be. Sex is one thing—and with you, a fucking really good thing—but it can't be more than that. And most importantly, I need to know that when either of us is ready to call...this off, we'll still be friends. If not—if we can't still have our relationship—then I'm not willing to risk it with sex. I won't risk it."

A pit yawned open inside her, a deep, dark abyss. Bitterness mixed with hurt, but she swallowed it down. He liked having sex with her, but nothing else. Not her heart. Just her friendship and her body.

"So friends with benefits. That's what you're saying," she

said, the even tone revealing nothing of the chaos swirling in her chest.

"I suppose so, yes. And," he added, shaking his head, "this stays between us. No confiding in Renee or Sophia. And I won't tell Ronin, Zeph, or Jason. We both know none of them would approve considering what happened between Renee and Jason. We would have to keep it our secret. And when it ends, no one knows, no one is hurt."

When it ends... Because, she knew, there was no doubt in his mind that it would eventually be over.

He folded his arms on the stone top. "Can you handle that, Tenny? Because if you can't, if that's not something you want, then we never fuck again and remain just friends. We forget about today and move on like we have been."

As if it could be that easy. For her, the strongest bleach couldn't ever erase those hours from her brain. Couldn't scrub the ghost of his touch from her body.

That he could if she didn't agree to his terms let her know she couldn't afford to become more emotionally invested than she was. And she damn sure couldn't admit her love to him again. Ask him for more. Not when he just told her that could never be.

She inhaled.

Okay, so she couldn't have all of him. But, if she accepted his...bargain, she could take as much of him as he was willing to give. And then walk away. Her heart and pride intact.

"I have a job interview Thursday," she said.

He stared at her, his expression a little stunned, but then full of *what the fuck*. What? Had he thought she'd forgotten about quitting as his PA?

"A job interview," he repeated. "When did this happen?" He shook his head, holding his hands up. "Screw it. I don't want the details."

"I'm not telling you to hurt you," she said, her voice

softening. She flexed her fingers, the urge to reach for him instinctive, but instead, she curled them into a fist. "I want to let you know that I can handle it. I'm getting my own life, Dom. You don't have to protect me. Or worry about me clinging to you or raging about broken promises when the sex ends."

Yeah, she'd unfortunately been on hand to witness one or two of those dramatic, embarrassing episodes with women he'd tried to gently let down. Even though, knowing how he hated relationships, she doubted he'd *ever* uttered vows of undying devotion or commitment to them.

"You're right; I do know you better than anyone," she continued. "It just so happens that when I eventually enter a relationship with a man, I want someone whose end game is love. I eventually want what Zeph and Sophia have, and I more than anyone realize that man will not be you. So no commitment, no hope-filled fantasies that sex will turn into monogamy. Deal?"

Relief and another, unidentifiable emotion crossed his face. But before she could decipher it, he cocked his head to the side. "Are you sure?"

"Yes, I'm sure," she scoffed. "I'm a big girl."

Look at you taking me. I knew you could.

His praise from that morning echoed in her head, stroking over her skin, skimming her nipples, and gliding between her legs like a phantom hand. A big, calloused hand with long, elegant fingers. He lifted his crystal blue eyes to hers. And she watched them darken to a shadowed navy. Maybe the same memory had leaped in his head, too.

"Come here," he commanded, lust tearing his voice up like freshly churned gravel on a pitted road. For a second, she didn't move. Couldn't move as a flash of doubt flickered inside her. Was she doing the right thing? Would she be able to walk away as she believed?

"Changed your mind already?" Dom asked, studying her with a hooded stare.

Changed her mind? She took a few precious seconds to analyze her heart, the sensations popping and crackling through her like a live, electrical current in the rain. Oh, no. With the heat of lust already rising inside her, she hadn't changed her mind.

She couldn't.

She circled the island, and he rose from the stool. They stared at one another, the low hum of the oven the only sound in the kitchen. Slowly, he lowered his head, and she rose on her toes, meeting his mouth halfway. He brushed his lips over hers, giving her a proper greeting. Then, with a low rumble of pleasure, he burrowed the fingers of both hands in her hair, holding her steady for the thrust of his tongue. God, his kiss. Already, his taste was familiar, addictive. And as she tilted her head, deepening the merger of their mouths, the kiss was fast becoming something she craved.

Desire rippled through her, and a greedy whimper escaped her. His head jerked up, and he studied her, the weight of it intense. Did he see the need that lit her like a torch, that warmed her face?

"Damn," he swore, low and harsh as he turned her around and flattened her palms on the island.

"I think this might be your favorite position," she teased, glancing over her shoulder as she widened her stance and arched her back. Lifted her ass toward him.

Groaning, he undid her jeans, shoved them down along with his sweatpants and gripped his dick, stroking the length from the base to the head. She felt her eyes widen at the unashamedly carnal, hedonistic display. Pleasure shot down her spine, and her already damp folds grew wetter. She grew hotter.

"Please," she begged.

His gaze rose from the flesh between her thighs to her face. Without preamble, he shifted forward and sank inside her. Not stopping until his balls pressed against her flesh.

Her chin dropped, and all she could do was moan. And shake. And demand... "Oh God. *More.*"

His forehead pressed to her shoulder blade, and he wrapped his arms around her, slipping a hand between her legs to seek out her clit. She rocked back into him as he circled and rubbed, her core squeezing him like a fist.

"That's where you're wrong," he growled, setting up a slow thrust and grind. "With you, they're all my favorite."

That was the last thing she heard for a while.

Chapter Eleven

"Explain to me why I agreed to this lunch again?" Tennyson muttered as they entered the upscale eatery in the Westlake neighborhood of Seattle. Brian Yates, Dom's agent, had chosen the popular restaurant where, at any given time, local rock artists, politicians, dealmakers, and Seattle's football elite could be seen.

"Appearances. It's all about appearances," Dom drawled, quoting Brian's motto. In the last seven years while Brian had been Dom's agent, Tenny had learned it was just one of many coined phrases he liked to echo. Each one seemed more pretentious and pompous than the last.

She sighed. Okay, so she should probably ease up on the sports agent. After all, it was his job to make sure Dom received and signed the best contract offers, handle Dom's business and endorsement deals, as well as manage his money. And Brian was damn good at what he did. But…his big, good ol' boy smile, booming voice, and gregarious manner hid the mind of a shark. Most people only saw the wide, amicable grin he usually wore. Tennyson looked into his gray eyes and glimpsed the cold machinations of a man constantly working an angle.

Then there was the fact that he couldn't seem to figure out that her face wasn't located in her breasts. She frowned. Since she would be attending lunch with Dom, maybe his gaze would remain above her neck.

"And because I asked you to," Dom answered her question, his palm warm and reassuring on the small of her back.

"Oh right," she grumbled.

"Hey." He stopped in the center of the foyer, halting her with a touch to her hip. The maître d' moved from behind the reservations stand and headed in their direction, but Dom didn't spare the tall, thin man dressed in all black a glance. All of his attention remained focused on her, and she fought not to fidget under all that intensity. God, those eyes could pierce right through her. "I know you said before that sometimes Brian makes you uncomfortable. If you're really that uneasy, I can take this lunch by myself and meet up with you later at the house. I don't want you to feel pressured into staying."

After a brief hesitation, she shook her head. "No, I'm good."

And she was; she could've said no when Dom invited her along. But that internal clock ticking away inside her head reminded her that not only was her time with him as lovers on a countdown, but so were the days or weeks she had left in Seattle. If the interview went well tomorrow, she would be one step closer to moving thousands of miles away. She didn't want to waste one second. If Dom wanted her with him, then she was going to the damn lunch.

But she'd keep her fork handy in case an unwanted hand traveled too close.

"You sure?" he pressed.

"I'm sure," she insisted. "Now let's go before the nudnik rings your phone off the hook looking for you."

She shifted forward, smiling at the hovering maître d'. After a moment, Dom followed, his palm resuming its former position on her lower back. "Yeah, well, try not to call him a pest to his face," he muttered in her ear.

Before Dom could give the host his name, the man beamed. "Welcome to The Terrace, Mr. Anderson. Your party is waiting for you. Please allow me to show you to your seat."

"Thanks," Dom replied with a nod of his head.

His demeanor reflected nothing of the orphaned foster kid from Dayton, Ohio, who'd attended a state university on a scholarship. In his light brown sports coat, white button-down, and dark gray pants, he exuded elegance, wealth, and sophistication. Even the medium-length, tousled hair brushing his jaw didn't detract from the image; it added a sexy confidence that had always been there before the football contracts, media spotlights, and razor commercials. It didn't surprise her at all that heads of men and women turned as he strode through the restaurant with a grace that was both athletic and sensual.

You're staring, her smug, bitchy inner voice taunted. She snatched her gaze from Dom's strong profile and trained it on the spectacular view of Lake Union ahead of her through one of the three walls made up entirely of glass. At least if she was staring at the beautiful water, charming houseboats, and the colorful homes dotting the shore, she could appear less...taken.

When she'd agreed to Dom's offer of a no-strings, friends-with-benefits arrangement yesterday, it'd been a no-brainer. After all, other than the sex, what he proposed wasn't so different than what she'd been doing for the past decade: pretending she wasn't in love with him; settling for friendship.

Now they were just screwing like rabbits. She could handle it.

No sweat.

And, this morning, if she'd had to shore up the cracks and holes last night had knocked in her emotional shield like a wrecking ball, then to finally be in his arms had been worth it. She only had to continue the charade for a little while longer.

"I was just about to call you," Brian said by way of greeting, rising from the table and dragging her back into the present. He shook Dom's hand and tugged him into one of those back-slapping hugs men who weren't really close did. That salesman smile didn't waver as he turned to greet her, but it did tighten a bit around the edges. "Tennyson. How good to see you again. I didn't know you were joining us today."

She extended her arm before he could even consider drawing her close. Not that he would dare "accidentally" touch her while Dom stood there to witness it. Still, better to be safe than sorry.

"I invited her along," Dom answered smoothly, pulling out a chair for her. Once she was seated, he lowered into the one beside her, his thigh brushing hers. "Hope it's not a problem." His tone suggested it better not be a problem. She cringed. So subtle.

"Not at all. Not at all," Brian assured him. "I'm always delighted to see our Tennyson."

She struggled not to roll her eyes.

"I'll send your server right over to take your orders. My name is Raymond," the maître d' said. "If you need anything at all, please don't hesitate to ask." With a deferential nod, he backed away from the table, and not less than ten seconds later, a waiter in a spotless white shirt and black pants appeared beside their table.

"Good afternoon. My name is Anthony, and I have the pleasure of serving you today." He proceeded to ramble off the chef's special dishes of the day along with the wines paired with the meals. Once he paused, they placed their orders. Assuring them they'd chosen well, he disappeared.

"Well, I spoke with the editor at *Sports Unlimited*. They would like to do an interview including a full photo spread…" Brian set his iPad on the table and started the meeting.

The next forty-five minutes passed in a blur of conversation covering possible endorsement deals, preliminary negotiations about Dom's next contract with the Warriors, and various interviews for the next few weeks. Tennyson recorded notes about the interview dates in her iPad. She wouldn't be working for Dom by the time the last two events took place, but she needed to pass along the information to her replacement. If they could ever find one. That reminded her… She jotted down a memo in red for Thursday after her telephone interview for the position in Dayton. As soon as it was over, she would be pulling out the qualified applicants in the next batch of résumés.

"…So I've arranged with her agent to have you escort her to the Los Angeles movie premiere. Let me tell you, she was *very* excited." Brian chuckled, picking up his glass of wine.

Tennyson jerked her head up just as Anthony set a plate of crème brûlée in front of her. Escort? Premiere? She'd been so lost in thought over how to trick Dom into choosing a new personal assistant, she'd zoned out on the conversation. And had apparently missed Brian trying to hook him up with a starlet.

Her stomach bottomed out, but nausea quickly rushed in to fill it. Fixing her gaze on the delicate dessert and lush fruit, she didn't dare look at Dom. What could she say? *I don't want you to go on a date with this actress who probably makes Charlize Theron look like Quasimodo.* Their arrangement didn't include exclusivity or demands on each other. She wouldn't have objected before yesterday; she couldn't today.

Though *no!* scraped at the back of her throat, she deliberately scooped up the heavy cream. The rich dessert might as well have been a mouthful of ashes. She tasted nothing but the hurt she had no business feeling.

"Pass," Dom said.

She snapped her attention from the crème brûlée to Dom, and both she and Brian gaped at him. *What?*

The agent slowly lowered his glass to the table, his eyes slightly narrowing before he shook his head, a "c'mon" smile curving his lips. "Dom, this is the supporting actress in a movie that already has Oscar buzz. You can't buy this kind of publicity. Look what Gisele did for Tom. Made them a super couple in the world of sports, raising both their profiles. Two beautiful superstars together? People eat that kind of thing up."

"No." His flat refusal brooked no argument. "I'm not arm candy for anyone."

Brian scoffed. "Since when? What about the actress from that superhero flick?"

"Brian, let. It. Go," Dom stated, and Tennyson stiffened at the steel edging the flat tone.

"Fine, fine," the other man relented, throwing his hands up in the age-old sign of surrender. "Whatever you say. I'll let her agent know."

"Good." Silence hung over the table, and it vibrated with tension. A low buzz broke the quiet, and Dom pulled his cell from his pocket. After a quick peek, he stood. "Sorry. This is Coach. Be right back."

He moved away from the table, leaving her with Brian. She filled her mouth with more of the dessert, studying the blueberries and strawberries dotting the plate.

"So, you're fucking him."

Shock rippled through her in icy waves. Her spoon clattered to the dish. Brian contemplated her, a sleek, dangerous cat ready to pounce, its tail slowly swishing back and forth.

"C'mon now, don't bother trying to deny it." He propped his elbows on the arms of his chair and steepled his fingers under his chin. "It's pretty obvious. You two have always been close *friends*," he said, giving "friends" an ugly emphasis, "but today something's changed between you. You're sitting closer. He's even more solicitous than usual. There's a tension here," he wagged a finger back and forth between her and Dom's empty chair, "that only exists between two people who are screwing."

"Whether we are or not is none of your business," she stated, relieved her voice didn't reveal how shaken his crude, blunt observation had left her.

"Oh see, that's where you're wrong," he objected, leaning forward, all semblance of the affable agent gone. In his place sat the flint-eyed shark who devoured weak prey. "When his personal relationships interfere with his career, it's completely my business. And you, Tennyson, have always been a distraction. From the very beginning. But now that you're having sex with my client, you're worse. You're a liability."

"What the hell are you talking about?" she snapped. Anger bubbled inside her like a geyser ready to blow. But underneath the rage lurked bruised pride and insecurity. Because Brian only voiced the worry and self-doubt that'd she'd lugged around for years.

She feared being a burden to Dom—emotionally, physically, financially. The terror of being a crippling responsibility to him haunted her like a ghost in her soul.

"Did Dom tell you I first approached him during his junior year at Ohio State about entering the draft? I was ready to take him on as a client, but he refused to leave college because he couldn't leave Ohio until you finished high school and aged out of the foster care system. Then, when he eventually did enter the draft a year later, he made sure more than half of his signing bonus went to pay for your college education instead of his own expenses. He hired you—an inexperienced kid—as his PA instead of the many highly qualified applicants I presented to him. Like I said, you've been a distraction when his main focus should be on the game and his career. Especially now, with the renewal of his contract coming up."

He shook his head, a subtle sneer curling a corner of his mouth. "And now, he's turning down appearances that will make him even more of a household name and put him firmly in the eyes of the public who don't know a first down from going down. He's never had an issue with being on the arm of a beautiful woman before, so the problem has to be you. Now that you're in his bed, he's even more emotionally involved and turning down priceless opportunities. You're a liability, Tennyson. And if you really cared for Dom, you would walk away, let him lead his life, let him be great without an albatross weighing him down."

Each word smacked her harder than the previous one. She tried to deflect, to justify each point he hurled at her. Like Dom wasn't more emotionally involved with her just because they'd added sex to their friendship. A condition of their... arrangement was no emotional entanglements. But, she couldn't deny that Dom had agreed to similar engagements in the past where he accompanied an actress or model to an event. Had she not been able to hide her discomfort, and he'd turned it down in deference to her feelings?

You're a liability.
Let him be great without an albatross weighing him down.
If you really cared for Dom, you would walk away.

The accusations sliced through her, leaving her heart, her conscience, and her pride in ribbons littering her feet.

Was that how everyone saw her? A little lost puppy trailing after him, begging and happy for the scraps he kindly threw at her? A hindrance that held him back from reaching his full potential, not just on the field but in the business of football?

All this time, she'd protested to Dom about needing to live her own life, walk her own path. The irony that he could've been thinking the same thing for years, that he could've had his own life and made different choices if not burdened by her, twisted her stomach into knots.

Dom's rule had been clear—nothing changed between them just because they were sleeping together, and they would remain unencumbered and friends. But things were already changing, just as Brian pointed out.

"Sorry about that," Dom said, returning from his phone call. He dropped into his seat, sliding an arm along the back of her chair.

"Everything okay?" Brian inquired, his scrutiny briefly dropping to the proprietary half embrace.

"Yeah, just something about practice tomorrow." Dom cupped her shoulder and squeezed. "You good?" he murmured.

She forced a smile, hoping it didn't reflect the turmoil and confusion whirling inside her head like a cyclone. "I'm fine."

Dom studied her for several long moments, and she met the piercing gaze that she sometimes swore had X-ray vision capabilities. Seconds later, he must've been satisfied by what he glimpsed—or what she allowed him to glimpse—because he nodded.

Brian shifted the conversation back to deals, contracts, and upcoming events.

And she tried to pretend that the curdling in her stomach was because of the dessert's richness and not due to the uneasy sense of foreboding that she and Dom had committed a huge mistake.

Chapter Twelve

Dom closed the front door of his house behind him, his attention completely focused on the woman walking toward the staircase. He narrowed his gaze on the straight line of her back, the tense set of her shoulders, the stiff gait that replaced her usual fluid, relaxed manner. If she were facing him, he'd bet his Wonder Woman coffee mug that the skin above the bridge of her nose would be wrinkled with a small frown.

For a woman who had trouble expressing her feelings, she was shit at concealing her thoughts and emotions.

And since he'd returned from his phone call with Coach Declan during lunch an hour ago, she'd been quiet. Too quiet. Something was bothering her, and so far, she'd refused to confide in him. But Tennyson could duck and dodge with the best of them, and he didn't have the patience to wait her out.

"What's wrong?" He trailed her up the stairs, his longer legs eating up the distance between them in several strides. Once she cleared the last step and stood on the second floor, he grasped her elbow, halting her. She stiffened in his hold as he tried to turn her around, but after a moment, she stopped resisting. Pinching her chin, he inched her head up so her eyes were studying him instead of his Adam's apple. "What's wrong, Tenny? And don't tell me nothing. I know that's woman-speak for shit's about to hit the fan," he teased.

But she didn't roll her eyes or even lay into him about being a meathead sexist. Instead, she remained silent, confirming his suspicion.

"Talk to me, sweetheart," he murmured.

"You shouldn't call me that," she replied.

Frowning, he rubbed a thumb over her full lower lip. "Call you what?"

"Sweetheart. And you shouldn't do that, either." She jerked out of his grasp and stepped back from him.

"Tennyson, what the hell?" Irritation flashed inside him. If only God had blessed men with the ability to read a woman's mind. Because they were damn confusing. "You want to tell me what that's supposed to mean? I can't come near you now and can only call you by your name?"

"We have an agreement. Nothing changes between us except for having sex. Before, you wouldn't have called me sweetheart or touched my mouth. So don't do it now."

He shifted forward, eliminating the space she'd inserted between them. The irritation deepened, stirring into a simmering anger. This—whatever was going on—was about more than his stipulation on the benefits aspect of their bargain. He hadn't forgotten it. Hell, he'd been reminding himself of his own rules all morning.

The protectiveness that had always been a part of him when it came to Tennyson had somehow magnified between yesterday and today, evolving into a possessiveness that would've made his caveman ancestors knock their clubs together in approval. He'd invited Tennyson with him to lunch because he wanted to spend his day off with her, even if it meant sharing a couple of hours with Brian. But when they'd arrived at the restaurant and Brian's scrutiny had passed over her, lingering just a bit damn too long on her legs and breasts, he'd had to strangle the urge not to snap his longtime agent in half like one of those dry sesame-seed pretzel sticks on the table.

This need for her left him reeling in a mixture of lust and disquiet. Even now, what she said made sense. But he wanted to kick a hole in the wall she'd thrown up, battering it until she let him in. Until she didn't hide anything from him.

The conflicting emotions were a red penalty flag thrown on the field of his own private battle. Caution. Back away. Emotionally and physically.

Moving back and granting them both breathing room, he thrust his fingers through his hair, glancing away from her. The temptation of her. Because though she'd instructed him not to caress her, he hadn't suddenly gone spontaneously blind. He couldn't *not* stare at the lush curves or imagine his tongue sliding between them. Couldn't *not* meet her dark chocolate eyes and not see them glazing over with passion.

Cursing under his breath, he exhaled and wrestled the jumbled thoughts and runaway desire under control. Control. Shit. He'd become known for his cold focus and exacting discipline. Tennyson twisted all that into a joke. "Let's start over. What's bothering you?"

"You," she accused, shoving her curls out of her face. "What was that at lunch?"

"What. Was. What?" He grabbed a hold of his rapidly dwindling patience.

"You turned down the movie premiere without even a second thought."

Hold on. She was pissed over *that*? What the fuck? He shook his head. "I didn't want to go."

"You haven't had any problem going to those types of events before…before…" She waved a finger between them.

"So why now, Dom?"

"Okay, let me get this straight," he said slowly, confusion and anger coalescing into a swirling, murky mass in his chest. "You *wanted* me to go out on a date with another woman." Even stating it sounded asinine and just fucking weird to his ears.

"What I wanted or didn't want shouldn't have mattered. It never did any other time. And that's the point," she retorted in the same I'm Talking to a Crazy Person tone he'd used.

"Are you— Wait." Her words penetrated his skull, and full comprehension bloomed. Cocking his head to the side, he studied her, eyes narrowed. A hard pulse of lust and something deeper—scarier—throbbed in his lower stomach. "It mattered to you before that I went with those women?"

Surprise flashed in her gaze before a shutter seemed to drop over her face and voice. "No," she said, tone flat. "Why should it?"

He shook his head slowly. "You're lying. Again." He could tell.

You would be surprised at how good I am at hiding things.

She'd uttered those words to him yesterday. Then, he'd denied that she would ever be able to keep anything from him. Not with her shitty lying skills.

Now he was starting to believe her.

Emitting a sound that could've been a groan or strangled scream, she glared at him. "Don't try to deflect, Dom. Before we had sex, you wouldn't have thought twice about letting Brian arrange the date and public appearance. Hell, you would've probably found a way to scrape up tickets for me."

"So you not only want me to go on a date with another woman, you want to go and watch, too." He nodded as if that shit made sense.

"Don't be ridiculous," she snapped.

"This whole thing is ridiculous," he snapped back, his

temper frayed. "Now why don't you cut the bullshit and tell me what's really on your mind."

"Football is your top priority. It always has been, always will be. But today, you made a decision that was counteractive to that. And you did it for me. For my feelings," she almost shouted. She reeled back slightly, her eyes widening as if her outburst had surprised her, too. Yes, too. Because she'd shocked the shit out of him.

His gut instinct reaction was to deny her accusation. But he paused, and it hit him that she was correct. He had to compartmentalize. If this friends-with-benefits, no-strings-attached arrangement was going to work and their friendship be intact afterward, then he had to remember his priorities. The end game. Which was football. Always football. Security. Legacy. A path to another career after he hung up his jersey. Plus, he just loved the game itself.

"You're right. No, don't look away from me," he admonished, gently cupping her cheek. He waited until her gaze returned to his. Christ, she was so fucking pretty. "I did make the decision based on your feelings, and yeah, there is a chance I would've agreed to go before you and I started having sex. But I also turned it down because I didn't want to touch another woman while I have you." This time he not only swept his thumb over her bottom lip, he dipped the tip into her mouth, grazing his skin along the edge of her teeth. The abrasive sensation echoed along his cock, and it didn't take much imagination to envision her teasing his flesh with that same hint of pleasure/pain. "So I'll promise not to confuse things again. For both our sakes. But I'm adding another stipulation to our deal. Don't expect me to fuck another woman when I'm with you."

She scoffed, turning away from him. Or trying to. He didn't allow it. "You can't possibly know you won't want someone else. You forget I've seen the women you've screwed with my own eyes. You don't make a habit of denying yourself..."

"I don't think with my dick. It pisses me off that you believe I'm not capable of saying no. And that once more you're comparing yourself to other women. Do I have to remind you of our lesson from yesterday?" he pressed, the greedy bastard inside him hoping she'd say yes. Just the memory of how he'd educated her—of how she'd responded—had his balls tightening and dick hardening until it pressed against his zipper.

"No," she breathed. "No reminder necessary."

"That's a shame." Unable to prevent himself any longer, he dipped his head for a quick taste of her lush mouth. He groaned. And returned for another sample. Sweetness of the wine she'd had with lunch. Richness of the creamy dessert. And her. All her. "For now, my dick isn't getting hard for anyone else. I'm not thinking about tomorrow, or some faceless woman. You. You're who I see when I fuck my fist. You're who I want down on her knees, lips stretched wide around my cock."

He circled her mouth with his finger, his gut pulling tight with the too-graphic image. "You're who I want to ride, bareback. Fuck, do you know how it felt to be inside you, with nothing between us? Like goddamn heaven. And hell. Everything beautiful and painful. Pleasure and agony. Yeah, being balls deep in you is like nothing in this fucking world." He abandoned her cheek and tunneled his fingers into the dark, wild curls that somewhere along the line he'd developed a probably unhealthy fascination with. Gripping her hair, he tugged her head back. Watched her lashes flutter. Heard her soft, hungry gasp. "I want it again," he growled against her mouth. "Are you going to give it to me?"

A moan escaped her seconds before she lifted those lashes. "Yes."

"For however long I want it?" he demanded.

The haze that had started to cloud her eyes slowly sharpened. "For however long *I* want it."

A dark, hot lust slid through his veins, slow and heavy, pouring right into his cock. "There she is," he praised, loosing a low chuckle. "There's my Tennyson."

My Tennyson. A glimmer of panic flickered inside him at the possessiveness in the claim. The claim. That, too, gave him pause. Or should've. But lust overrode the warning, and he covered her mouth, his tongue pushing forward, and she met him with an eager parry and thrust. The kiss was a raw, messy, prolonged battle, peppered with groans and her sexy whimpers. Fingers curled into his shirt, she rose on her toes, opening her mouth wider, offering him more. And he wasn't a fool; he took it. Took it all.

With another of those greedy sounds, she tore her mouth from his and nipped a stinging path down his chin, jaw, and neck. With movements that spoke of impatience and need, she attacked the buttons on his shirt. Good. He didn't help her; he loved this side of her—hot, hungry, forceful. It let him know he wasn't the only one caught up in this crazy, disorienting lust.

Her soft, wicked tongue licked at his collarbone, tracing it, and he tilted his head back, granting her more access to him. Jesus, her touch. It seared him. Tomorrow, he wouldn't be surprised if he found scorch marks on his skin. Not when every caress and small bite branded pleasure into him. Her teeth lightly scored his chest, grazed his nipple. He lifted his head, the urge to watch a fevered compulsion.

"Harder, sweetheart," he muttered. "Mark me." He wanted to glance down his body tomorrow and see the proof that she'd had him.

Sighing, she sucked on him, lapping at the flat, dark brown peak before capturing it between her teeth and tugging.

Pleasure rode the edge of pain, and he clenched his jaw, fighting the urge to whip her dress over her head and drive his cock into the heated, giving flesh between her legs. She wasn't gentle, didn't go easy on him, just as he'd demanded. When she switched to the other nipple, he almost objected, craving more of her special brand. But then she closed her mouth over him again, teasing the other nub to a hard point that she tortured with lips, tongue, and teeth.

Yanking the shirttails from the band of his pants, she glanced up at him, her mouth swollen and damp. The full, plump curves beckoned him, and he lowered his head, drawing her up his body. But she resisted, spreading the sides of his shirt wide and stroking her palms up his abdomen, over his chest, to his shoulders. She stared at him, her gaze almost...reverent. He'd been called hot, gorgeous, eye candy, and all other labels that meant women found him attractive. And he'd smiled and deflected, the compliments rolling off his back. But in this moment, with her eyes gleaming, and her breath breaking on her lips every time she swept her fingertips over his inked skin, he felt...beautiful. Worthy of the appreciation lighting her dark eyes.

And fuck, didn't that sound like he'd grown a vagina in the last five-point-two seconds.

Emotion doesn't have a place here. He grasped onto the reminder like it was a lifeline in a shark-infested ocean. Submerging the tenderness beneath the lust, he gripped her hips and hauled her forward, grinding his throbbing cock into the soft plane of her belly. She was so petite, sometimes he wanted to be gentler, more careful. But he couldn't. She... incited something primal, raw, almost crude inside him. He wanted—needed—to get dirty with her. Get covered in her. Sink inside her...go down and never come back up for air. Who the fuck needed air when he could drown in her scent, her taste, *her*?

Not that she seemed to desire gentle or careful. No, the harder he tugged on her hair...the firmer he held her... the faster and more powerful his thrusts into her body, the wetter, hotter, wilder she became. This woman didn't mind how deep or dark he got; she craved it.

Craved him.

Eyes on his, she slowly unbuckled his belt and undid his pants. His lungs stuttered, then pumped faster, working overtime as she slid her hand inside and cupped him over his boxer briefs.

"Damn it, Tenny," he growled, bucking into her grip. Lust slammed into him, a sledgehammer rocking him back on his heels. He braced himself, spreading his thighs wider. Hell, just one squeeze, and she had him ready to blow like a preteen watching his first porno. Her fist stroked him, going up his length and pausing on the head, then retreating. Air rushed from him, and he forced himself to remain still under her unhurried exploration.

"I've never had any desire to take a man in my mouth. But with you, it's all I've been thinking about," she murmured with another glide of her fist. "How you'll taste. How you'll feel. If I'll be able to take all of you."

What? He could barely hear over the rushing of blood in his ears and the pleasure singing a goddamn aria in his veins. But when her words penetrated, shock and a primitive Me-Tarzan-You-Jane satisfaction and possessiveness swelled inside him, almost shoving aside the lust. Almost.

"You going to let me be the first to fuck this pretty mouth?" he rasped, tracing her lips with a fingertip. She nodded, and he groaned, slipping three fingers past her teeth. Immediately, her tongue greeted him, curling around him. "So pretty," he whispered as she licked at his fingers as if she were already on her knees swallowing his dick. In her fist, his flesh pounded like an anvil. His gut clenched, desire rushing so hot and hard, it was almost punishing.

She gave his fingers one last lick, then, bending her knees, trailed her lips down his chest and abs.

"Wait." The order was harsher than he intended, but she straightened, her attention fixed solely on him. He shrugged out of his jacket and open shirt, nearly tearing the items off him and tossing them to the floor. The woman who'd helped him choose the $300 sports coat would probably stroke out to see him throw it at his feet for Tenny to kneel on. But he couldn't think of a better use.

As she sank to her knees in front of him, he once more tangled his hands in her gorgeous, untamable curls. Jesus, he might have developed an obsession with them. Their wildness that reflected the passion he'd been blind to until recently. The soft and coarse texture that reflected her delicacy and strength. Their beauty that others might find unconventional but he found to be just...her.

He sucked in a breath as she tugged down the front of his boxer briefs and, closing her fist around his dick, pulled him free. Her sigh along his sensitive, taut flesh had him choking back a groan. The way she stared at him—as if his cock were one of those shiny, new culinary gadgets that excited her but she had yet to figure out how to use... His stomach muscles contracted, his abs in stark relief as he waited for her to figure him out. He didn't rush her, exerting a control that would've made his performance on the football field laughable. The need to push his hips forward, part her lips, and sink into her mouth clawed at him. But he fought the urge, letting her take the lead, have him at her own speed and pleasure.

He was a goddamn saint.

His cock appeared almost brutish in her small hand, but she could take him. Just like she had last night. He stared, every bit of him concentrated on her lips drawing closer and closer to his throbbing flesh. *Take it, sweetheart. Take it.* The plea looped in his head like a desperate chant. In this moment, he longed to be inside her mouth more than he coveted any winning season, award, or trophy.

Finally, fucking *finally*, she opened for him, took him inside, her heated warmth surrounding the swollen head. With a hum that vibrated around his dick, she swirled her tongue around the tip, lapping up the cum already easing out of him. Her lashes drifted down, hiding her gaze from him, but for once, he didn't demand she look at him. The slashes of red over her cheekbones, the hungry sounds she probably wasn't even aware of making telegraphed everything he needed to know. She loved this as much as he did. Yeah, maybe not as much. Her sweet mouth suctioning his cock, her tongue sliding along his length—it was a purgatory he never wanted to escape.

Her head bobbed up and down, her cheeks hollow from the strong suck she gifted him with. One hand fisted the bottom half of his cock, pumping and covering what her mouth couldn't take. Each wet glide, each earthy moan, each ravenous sweep of her tongue... Shit. She'd claimed to never have given head before. Any more "inexperienced," and she would kill him.

With a sigh, she lifted her head from him, licking him like one of her cake batter–covered spoons. And when she dipped her head lower, dragging a long, luxurious stroke over one of his balls before capturing it and drawing hard, he couldn't contain the animalistic growl that tore from him. His fingers dug into her scalp, and a part of him repudiated himself for being too rough, but that caveman part only she seemed to provoke in him had broken free, and there was no wrestling him back into his civilized cage. Not with his balls in her mouth.

She trailed her lips back up his dick, pausing to brush a kiss over the tip. But he was far past that. Grip firm and unyielding, he held her steady as he pushed between her puffy, abused lips. Pleasure—ripping, ruthless, relentless pleasure—surged through him, setting every nerve ending on fire. A live wire. He'd turned into a live wire, and she was the conduit.

"Suck me, sweetheart. Pull me inside, and suck me like you mean it." The words, thick and running on top of one another, were little more than an unintelligible rumble in his throat.

But she must've understood because, lifting a hand to his balls and massaging the tight sac, she drew him farther into her, pushing forward on him until her lips bumped her pumping fist. Then she removed her hand, and *Christ*, she took more. The head nudged the back of her throat, and he forced himself not to jerk her forward that precious inch that would slip him into that narrow passage.

First time. First time. The reminder whispered through the frenzied, excited din in his head like a silvery vein of reason. As close to the edge she shoved him, as surely as she stripped him of the veneer of civility, he could never forget who knelt before him, torturing him with a mouth that should have a Surgeon General warning slapped on it.

Tennyson.

Tenny.

With the question of his sanity ringing in his ears, he slowly pulled free of her, and gently guided her to her feet.

"Why didn't you finish?" she objected, and the hoarse quality to her voice that was a result of his cock in her mouth almost had him pushing her back to her knees. "Didn't you...?"

She didn't complete the question, but she didn't need to. Crushing his mouth to hers, he plunged his tongue in the mouth that had just damn near driven him mad. "If I'd liked it any more, I might be brain dead," he muttered against her lips. "But I want to come inside you. Deep inside." With her convulsing around him.

He glanced at the stairs, then down the hall. His room on the first level was too far; even those few moments of descending the staircase seemed too long to wait. Engulfing her hand in his, he led her down the hall to her room. In seconds, he had her stripped, on the bed, and his head buried between her thighs. Not until her thighs shook around his shoulders and her screams bounced off the walls did he stand and remove the rest of his clothes.

Stroking his cock, he climbed back on the mattress and studied the bare, glistening, swollen folds and the tiny entrance that would soon stretch around him. Damn, she was lovely. Though his flesh ached and throbbed, he couldn't help stroking his hands up her soft, silken body. The contrast between his golden skin and her coffee-and-cream complexion struck him as lovely. Sensual.

Fascinated, he couldn't drag his gaze from his long fingers sweeping over her belly, up her heaving chest and trembling breasts. In all the years Tenny and he had been friends, he'd never really *seen* the two of them as different. They'd had too many similarities—foster children, broken but strong, fighters, survivors. But now, with them naked and vulnerable, he viewed their diversity as if through newly opened eyes. And she'd—they'd—never been more beautiful. More...perfect.

He trailed a hand over her shoulder, throat, and cupped her cheek while he slowly, deliberately thrust into her. Unlike last night, he didn't ease into her. His free hand cradled her hip, holding her steady as he disappeared inside her. And her snug, silken, drenched flesh gloved him, embraced him. The urge to close his eyes and just savor the tight clasp and welcoming ripple of her pussy sang through him like an erotic melody. But he battled it, the need to keep his stare on the stretched entrance and folds taking him, accepting him even stronger. More vital.

Her hips rolled, meeting his every plunge with a passion that stole what little breath and lucidity he had left. What started as languorous and measured turned fierce, frantic, and so damn greedy. He planted a hand near her ear, preventing himself from crushing her. Pressing his forehead to hers, he recoiled and rocked his hips, slamming into her over and over, riding her hellbent for an ending that loomed so close but stretched so far away. An ending he wasn't even certain he wanted to reach. Not if it meant he couldn't continue burying himself in the sweetest heaven and the fieriest hell.

A bolt of electricity sizzled up his back, nailing him at the nape of his neck, before racing down again, and culminating in a sizzling current at the base of his spine. Gritting his teeth against the oncoming release, he reached between their bodies and rubbed her clit, circling the hard nub before gently pinching it.

A scream ripped from Tenny's throat as she went rigid, arching in a perfect bow. Her walls spasmed around his cock, sucking him deeper, milking him. Grabbing her hips, he rocketed into her, a growl rumbling in his chest. His mind blanked, and he was an animal with his mate, fucking her—them—into oblivion.

His hoarse shout razed his throat raw as he bucked against her, spilling into the flesh that had become his sole reason for being. He couldn't speak, hell, couldn't breathe as he pumped, chasing mind-shattering pleasure. And as his mind rebooted, and he eased his weight down on her, unwilling to separate from her, he pushed aside the thread of unease that had returned with his brain activity.

He should get up, give them space after that...whatever it'd been. But he couldn't. Instead, he curled his body around hers, inhaling her sweet musk of citrus and sex.

No commitment. No relationship. No changes. Just sex.

The mantra ran through his head, and for a second, he focused on mentally repeating it. But the warmth of her and the heavy satisfaction deadening his limbs submerged the reminder under unconsciousness.

Tomorrow. He'd reinforce the boundaries tomorrow.

• • •

"Seriously?" Tennyson demanded from the doorway of Dom's bedroom.

If not for the tray with freshly baked chocolate-chip cookies and two glasses of milk perched on it that she held, he could easily picture her fists propped on her hips as she glared at him.

"What?" he asked, throwing back the covers and jumping from the bed to retrieve the tray. Part of his motive was chivalry. And the other part was the aroma of those cookies. They were his damn weakness. He would have to work out extra hours in the gym to alleviate the guilt, but they were well worth the additional sweat and reps.

She jerked her chin in the direction of the television where clips from the previous week's football games scrolled along with the sportscasters' commentary. "Did you turn it on as soon as I left the room? Kinda makes me doubt my ability to drop you into a sexual coma."

Carefully setting the glasses on the bedside table nearest him, he flashed her a grin. "Sweetheart, never doubt your sexual prowess."

She snorted, climbing on the bed. "Prowess? Now who's busting out the vocab words?"

He chuckled and joined her on top of the covers, setting the tray with the cookies between them. He didn't hesitate to grab one and stuff the whole thing in his mouth.

"Damn, these are good," he mumbled.

"My cookies are always good," she deadpanned.

They glanced at each other and snickered.

Propping his back against the headboard, he passed her one of the glasses of milk and kept one for himself. The next twenty minutes passed in a comfortable, pleasant silence as they ate and watched television. After they were finished, he dragged on a pair of sweatpants and carried the empty dishes to the kitchen. By the time he returned, Tenny had snuggled under the blanket, and he paused, taken aback by the warmth swirling in his chest.

This wasn't the first time she'd curled up in his bed; he couldn't count the number of times they'd crashed here and watched movies. But then, he hadn't kissed that pretty mouth, sucked on those gorgeous breasts, or been inside her tight, little body. No, lying next to her now took on a whole new meaning. The impact of it was different. More powerful, more visceral.

A fine tension entered him, eating away at the particular ease and looseness that was a result of fantastic sex. It reminded him of the unease that had filtered through him earlier when she'd accused him of basing a business decision on her feelings. Then, he'd been determined to not lose focus on what had driven him, shaped him, and given him an identity all these years—football.

Maybe he needed that reminder again. Especially when the strings that he'd claimed to be nonexistent in their arrangement seemed to be tangling and growing tighter with each passing second.

"What's wrong?" she asked around a wide yawn.

Not immediately replying, he crossed the room and settled on the bed next to her.

"Do you know why I love football so much, Tenny?" he murmured, his stare fixed on the wide, arched window in his bedroom and the view of trees that had fully transformed into a gorgeous explosion of reds, oranges, and golds. After a moment, he didn't see autumn's display. A blurred, wavering picture of a big man with dark brown hair and a wide smile and a slender woman with red hair and laughing blue eyes had replaced it.

"No," she said, her voice and warmth closer. Her knee pressed into his thigh, and her citrus and sex scent drifted to him, teased him.

"My childhood was great," he said, images of that small but comfortable brick house in the middle-class neighborhood of Huber Heights flickering in his mind's eye. "My parents both worked to provide the best home for me, but they always had time for me. We had one steadfast rule in our house: dinner at the table every night. Didn't matter what we all had going on with work or school. We always ate as a family. That time was where we talked, laughed, reconnected. I never doubted for one second that I was loved by either of them."

He swallowed hard, attempting to dislodge the knot in his throat strangling him. His memories tended to overwhelm him, drown him. Which was why he didn't exhume them often. And by often, he meant ever. Not even to Tenny, though she knew the broad-brush strokes of his past.

"You can't live in Ohio and not love football," he continued, allowing a faint smile to curve a corner of his mouth. "And my family was no different. Especially my father. I learned the game before my ABCs. We attended every Friday night high school game, watched every college one on Saturday, and NFL on Sunday and Monday. Mom enjoyed it, too, but I think she got more of a kick out of watching us and just being together. Dad and I, though..." He shook his head, smiling. "We were fanatics. He had me enrolled in Pop Warner football as soon as I was old enough to join. Even then, I was good, fast, able to throw. I loved it. Loved everything about it. The best part, though, was knowing my parents were in the stands, cheering me on."

"They sound special. I knew they had to be even though you didn't talk about them," she whispered, her fingers intertwining with his, and he clutched them like a lifeline.

"Dad used to tell me I would play for the Bengals one day. That was the only thing we ever disagreed on. I wanted to be a Steeler." He laughed. "Football…it was our thing. Mom would get her crossword puzzles or true crime novels, Dad would have his two beers—no more than that—and Lay's plain potato chips, and I would have the ball he gave me when I was five. The three of us would sit in the living room and watch together."

He bowed his head, his heart pounding so hard that for a moment, he struggled to breathe. His fingers flexed as if trying to grasp something that was turning into elusive smoke and dust. And no matter how desperate, how frantically he swiped at it, grabbed at it, he could never capture it.

"One Saturday morning, my team faced our league's rivals. The game started at ten o'clock. We were kicking their asses. At half-time, I looked in the stands and couldn't find my parents. They always sat on the third row right behind our bench. At the end of the third quarter, they hadn't arrived. And when it ended, they still weren't there. They'd never missed a game. Not one. So when my coach approached me an hour later and told me there'd been a car accident and they'd died, a part of me wasn't completely shocked. I knew if they weren't there, it hadn't been by choice."

"Dom," she breathed, her voice catching. Her grip tightened on him, almost bruising. "I didn't know…"

"They died on their way to see me," he rasped.

"No." The objection cracked in the air like a whip. "They died doing what they loved. Supporting you. Cheering you on. Showing their love for you."

"You know," he said, hearing her words as if from a great distance, "I can't remember my mother's voice or my father's laugh anymore. Even the memory of how they looked becomes more blurred with each year. The social worker allowed me to keep pictures of them, but some of the kids in my first foster home thought it was funny to rip them up and leave them on my pillow. So I don't have anything of them but my fading memories and the connection we had through football. As long as I keep that connection, I'll never lose them."

"Dom, look at me."

He couldn't. Not with the pain so raw and fresh inside him like a wound with the scab torn off. Allowing her to see that... He shook his head. Hell, he didn't want to feel it; how could he let her stare it in the face?

But she didn't give him a choice.

With a gentle but firm grip on his chin, she turned his head toward her. She shifted, kneeling next to his hip, and for several long moments, she didn't say a word, just studied him, her eyes soft, dark, and gleaming with the tears that slowly rolled down her cheeks.

"Why are you crying?" he murmured, cupping her jaw and wiping away a tear with the pad of his thumb.

"Because you won't," she whispered. Turning into his hand, she kissed the heel of his palm, and the tender caress squeezed his heart in a tight fist.

Closing his eyes, he leaned forward until his forehead pressed to hers. His breath shuddered out of him, and he trembled. It embarrassed him how his body shook as if his skin and bones were too fragile to contain the churning of emotion swirling inside of him at category ten speed. And like objects directly in the path of those destructive winds, he was in danger of being swept up and flung away.

A sudden need to touch her surged within him, and he

didn't question it. Didn't fight it. He clutched her shoulders, dragged her to him, over him. In this black emotional storm, she grounded him. She was his anchor.

She didn't try to get him to talk as he jerked the T-shirt she'd slipped on over her head. She didn't utter an objection as he shoved down his sweatpants and freed his cock.

She did tunnel her fingers through his hair, cradling him, brushing her lips over his as he pushed deep, so fucking deep inside her. She did gasp and roll her hips, taking all of him as he whispered her name over and over against her mouth.

She did offer him oblivion.

And grateful, he took it.

Took everything.

Chapter Thirteen

Tennyson pressed her palms to the desk in Dom's home office, staring down at her spread fingers as if they contained the answers to the questions whirling around in her head.

Veronica Maitland with the Offices of Families and Children wanted her to come to Dayton for a face-to-face interview. She'd been very impressed with their telephone call and wanted to meet before the final decision was made. It was Wednesday, almost a week since she and Veronica had first spoken, and Tennyson had started to become nervous that maybe the other woman had changed her mind about Tennyson being a candidate for the job. But from the call she'd just received, that hadn't been the case at all.

Her belly clenched, and she sucked in a lungful of air and deliberately released it. Until an hour ago when she'd received the call, the job and relocation to Dayton had been "someday" and the future. Well, it seemed her future had become her near present.

She had to tell Dom. For weeks, she'd put off telling him about even applying for the position. And even though the morning after they'd first had sex, she'd mentioned the interview for a new job, she hadn't shared the exact details. All he knew was her time as his PA was ending. He had no clue she could possibly be moving across the country.

Closing her eyes, she covered her mouth, slowly rubbing it before sliding her hand down her chin.

A seed of doubt wormed its way inside her, taking root. Her reasons behind her decision hadn't changed. She needed to finally stand on her own, be her own safety net for the first time since they'd met. How could she ever know she was strong and independent if she always had Dom to fall back on? How could she ascertain who she was outside of him?

She'd had little control over her life. Her mother had shattered her confidence at an age when she'd needed affirmation and love most. Instead, her mother had turned Tenny into an object whose only purpose was obtaining attention. By the time Dom had come into her world, Tenny had felt like little more than a thing. His protection, affection, and devotion had slowly offered her an identity. He'd sheltered her, and she'd let him. She'd felt worthy only because that beautiful, fierce, gifted boy had loved her. She'd been content, if not happy, with his friendship even though a little more of her died each time he turned to a woman who wasn't her.

Now, that was no longer enough.

Actually, it hadn't been for a while. But adding sex to their relationship had brought it into crystal-clear focus. She'd burned under the heat of his passion, the brand of his possession. And there was no way in hell she could step aside and watch as another woman eventually claimed what she longed for as her own. It would destroy her, and her resentment and pain would destroy her and Dom.

And after his confession about his parents, she was more convinced than ever that she could never be a priority in his life. She knew what he'd been trying to tell her with that story. Football, his career, his drive to play and be number one, would always take precedence. Not that she could be angry with him—no, not after what he'd confided in her. For him, football was his last tenuous connection to the people who had loved him most. He hadn't said it, but she understood anyway: to lose it was to lose himself…to betray their memory.

How could she ever compete with that guilt, that desperation? A better question: should she?

Sighing, she swiveled in the desk chair and stared out the window. Heavy, brooding clouds clustered together, reflecting her mood. A foreshadow of the storm that would erupt between her and Dom. Because, yes, if they offered her the job, she would accept and move to Dayton. She would establish a new life, meet new friends, maybe welcome a new man into her life. A man who could love her as much as she did him. A man who could accept her vocabulary obsession, traumatic past, and fear of hospitals. A man who would place her first in his life, cherish her.

Though she'd made her decision, the unease squirming inside her didn't ease.

"Hey," Dom called from behind her.

She started, spinning around. Damn, she'd been so lost in her thoughts she hadn't heard the beeping of the alarm or him entering the office. Splaying her fingers over her chest like some faint-hearted damsel in distress, she stared at him. He must've showered at the facility because his dark hair was damp, and he wore his customary after-practice uniform of a long-sleeve thermal shirt and sweatpants. Even those simple clothes couldn't detract from his strength and vitality. Power emanated from him. Intensity radiated from his clear blue eyes, and she flushed under it. Images of them from the last several evenings fluttered across her mind—her riding him, their mouths fused together, sharing breath, coming together.

Unable to bear the scalpel-sharp force of that gaze, she ducked her head, pretending to organize the already organized desk.

"How was practice?" she asked, scrambling for some semblance of normalcy.

"It was fine." The short, vague reply relayed the truth, though. It must not have gone as well as that "fine" would have her believe. She swallowed a sigh. He worried so much about the game, his playing, and the backup quarterback watching him like a hawk. So much pressure weighed down those strong shoulders. And very soon, she would be adding more by announcing her intentions to leave. "What's going on? I had to call you a couple of times before you answered when I came in. Everything good?" He approached her, pressed a kiss to the top of her head, and then propped a hip on the desk's edge.

She could wave off his observation and postpone telling him about the job until later. Maybe after this week's game. At least wait until the weight of this coming Sunday had passed. The last thing she wanted was to be the source of a distraction.

And she was making excuses.

Shit.

"Actually, something came up that I need to talk to you about." She rose, unable to continue sitting still, and rounded the desk. "It's, uh, kind of important."

His eyes narrowed, but he shifted around so he faced her and remained silent, indicating for her to continue with a nod.

"Remember that job interview I told you about last week?" A flock of raptors took flight inside her chest, their wings battering her. Her pulse pounded, and a rush of white noise momentarily deafened her. Fear, acrid and metallic, coated her tongue. She'd never tasted it before in Dom's presence. "I heard back today, and they asked me to attend a second interview." She paused, a vise tightening around her throat. "In Dayton," she added in a low rasp.

The room filled with a frigid quiet that seemed to penetrate her bones, chilling her to the marrow. Outside, the first drops of rain bounced against the windows, the pitter-patter steadily growing in intensity. Each drum of water against glass emphasized the vacuum of silence in the room.

Helplessly, she stared at him, unable to tear her gaze away. His eyes, so clear seconds earlier, resembled the cloud-heavy sky she'd studied before he arrived. The full, sensual curves of his mouth hardened, firming into a grim line, and the chiseled line of his jaw could've been hewn from rock.

She didn't need to be inside his head to decipher his thoughts; they'd been friends too long for her not to understand what the anger stamped on his face meant. Pain. Confusion.

Betrayal.

Part of her yearned to shrink from the accusation in those hooded eyes, but she had to face this—face him—head on. The job, the conversation, the imminent separation—none of them were going away.

"This job opportunity is in Dayton," he stated, the flat intonation not fooling her. Not when her skin practically vibrated from the crackle of the emotional currents snapping between them.

"Yes. With the Offices of Families and Children for a Child Welfare Caseworker 1 position." She balled her fingers into fists at her side. Reaching for him, touching him even though she needed it so desperately would be a brutal mistake. "They want me to come to Dayton before making a final decision."

"When?" he asked in the same even tone. Ice slid through her veins.

"The Monday after next," she murmured.

"No, when did you decide to apply for a job in Ohio?"

She glanced away from him for the first time. How could she answer it truthfully without telling him *why* she'd chosen to submit for a position so far from Seattle...from him? She couldn't. Well, she couldn't and not admit how she'd loved him all these years. And confessing that wasn't an option. Still, premeditation wasn't only a sign of guilt in a court of law, but it'd be one in his eyes, too.

"About the time I told you about quitting," she hedged. "I didn't limit my job search to Seattle. And when Dayton came up, it just seemed like fate."

That much was true. It *had* seemed fortuitous, as if the often-fickle fate had taken pity and decided to throw her a bone.

"That was weeks ago. You've been lying by omission to me for *weeks*," he said, the first traces of anger leaking into his deep voice. "Letting me assume you were quitting to enter into social work here, in Seattle."

She couldn't deny his charge. Couldn't explain her actions because that would involve revealing her closest held secret. It would mean damaging their friendship beyond repair when he rejected her again. So she settled for, "I'm sorry."

He shook his head, the anger slowly bleeding away to leave a profound sadness that hurt as much as the whip in his voice had. "Why, Tenny? Why Dayton? There are plenty of jobs here."

The "with me" remained unspoken, but it wavered in the air between them. And wasn't that the irony? She could never be "with him." Another woman might one day have that privilege, but never her.

"The reasons I've given you from the beginning haven't changed, Dom," she said, risking taking a step toward him. "They're still true. And moving to Dayton seemed like coming full circle. It was their system that we grew up in that inspired me to pursue a social work degree."

"Never mind that you'll be thousands of miles away from home." Straightening, he stalked across the room, burrowing all ten fingers into his hair, clutching the strands in a tight grip.

After several long moments, he finally lowered his arms and lifted his head to meet her gaze. For the first time in their friendship, his eyes were shuttered, preventing her from glimpsing his emotions, his thoughts. She shivered and wrapped her arms around herself. The gesture didn't alleviate the sudden loneliness.

"Yes, but..." But what? It wouldn't change their relationship? Bullshit. Wasn't that one of the points of the cross-country move?

"Tell me, Tenny," he said, his voice a low rumble in the room. "Why does your getting your own life mean leaving mine?"

Sorrow and pain seized her, paralyzing her lungs. She couldn't speak, couldn't *breathe*. How couldn't he see she was fighting, *battling* inside? Grief, hurt, frustration, fear—the fury of them all were tearing her apart. God, how could he not know that leaving would rip her heart out? But so would staying. And in this instance, she had to put herself above everything—everyone—else. *Had to*. For her emotional survival, she had no other option but to choose herself.

"Give me a minute, okay?" he murmured, his gaze fixed on the window she'd stared out of only minutes earlier. "I need a little time."

Without a word, she rounded the desk and left the room, granting him the space he'd requested. Part of her thought, hoped, he would stop her. Ask her to sit down so they could finish discussing it, hash it out, and come to some sort of... conclusion. But he didn't.

Another first in their friendship.

Chapter Fourteen

"Red, thirty-two." The boom of his voice echoed in his helmet as he squared up behind the center and looked to his right, briefly making eye contact with Ronin. Then, he glanced to his left and repeated the cadence call so his second receiver as well as his linemen could hear the protection scheme. "Red, thirty-two. Set. Go! Go!"

The center snapped the ball, and Dom dropped back, scanning the field for his receivers. Spotting Ronin open, he launched the football. But just before his friend grabbed it, a safety appeared in front of Ronin and knocked the ball down. *Fuck*.

The sharp shrill of a whistle cut through the air, the piercing sound somehow indignant. All movement on the field halted as Coach Declan marched into the ordered chaos of the play. Sighing, Dom snatched off his helmet and dragged a hand through his hair, cursing under his breath. *Damn it*. This was practice, but if it'd been this Sunday's game against the Packers, his mistake could've resulted in a punt to the other team, or worse, Green Bay getting the ball.

"What the hell? All of you fucked up," Coach yelled. Pointing a finger at one of the offensive tackles, he spread his arms, palms up. "Jacobs. What the fuck are you doing? How're you going to let that end run free? You got to get your ass out the air and get over there. Dom, that was a bad read. You have to see that safety moving over. Get your goddamn head in the play. And for chrissakes…"

He continued the tirade, and Dom replaced his helmet, anger at himself a tight ball lodged in his chest. Ignoring the concerned looks both Zeph and Ronin aimed his way, he stalked back to his starting position and waited for Coach to finish.

Folding his arms, he stared straight ahead and tried to—how did Coach put it?—get his goddamn head in the play. His jaw clenched. Much easier said than done.

Yesterday, Tennyson had told him about the job offer…in Dayton. A muscle in his jaw twinged in protest.

It was a little over a week since he and Tennyson had first slept together and struck their new agreement. One would think, already being best friends, that sex would bring them closer. She was his closest confidante, handled the day-to-day operations of his life, had a permanent room in his home. Hell, he'd bought her cookware for his kitchen. The only thing they hadn't shared had been their bodies. So removing that last boundary, so to speak, shouldn't have been that big a deal. Yet, he couldn't have felt more distant from her.

No way could he cry foul about the sex. It was hot-as-hell, earth-shattering, what-the-hell-is-my-name-again sex, and she held nothing back from him when they were together. Totally uninhibited, raw, giving, and generous. Other women had preceded her, but he would be hard put to remember their names or faces. With her wild passion and innate sensuality, she rendered them forgettable. So yeah, he had no complaints about her as a lover.

No, that wasn't true.

His complaint was that he couldn't get enough. As soon as he had her, he craved her again, no matter that his body had waved the white flag of surrender. Apparently, his dick had a hit out on him.

But the easy fluidity and openness of their friendship… it'd changed.

Now he knew why.

Here he'd been wondering if she'd thrown up roadblocks to the intimacy they'd always shared because of something he'd done. Or maybe because she'd been worried about how it would affect them. The signs had been nothing overt; no, they were small things like a hesitation before answering what her plans were for the day. Or her refusal to spend nights with him in the kitchen he'd restored for her or the room he'd designated for her. Anyone knew that tiny dings and cracks soon became fissures and fractures that were much harder, sometimes impossible, to fix. Maybe he'd been fooling himself when he'd believed they could add sex to their relationship and still have one. Hell, at this point, he questioned if he could ever look at her and not see her naked, sweet body twisting and arching under his hands. Not see her dark brown eyes even darker with lust. Not see her coming apart, writhing on his cock.

And all along, her distance had been a result of her lying to him.

Not directly, but by omission. These past weeks, she'd been looking him in the face, sharing evenings with him, lying under him in his bed, and had been keeping a huge secret.

Of course, she might have remained quiet because of his aversion to her leaving. Even now, panic flared, that edgy feeling of a loss of control, of losing her. The rationalization of her reasons didn't stop the same, troubling agitation from settling inside him like an annoying pebble in a shoe. Didn't prevent the sense of powerlessness from gripping him and shaking him like a stick in the jaws of a dog.

In a week, she would be flying to Dayton, across the country. Away from him. Leaving him.

Like everyone else...

He scrubbed a hand over the back of his neck as if he could do the same to that small, dark voice that whispered against his skull.

He just couldn't shake the feeling that they would never be the same again.

And he had to get his head back in the game.

"All right. Run the play again," Coach called, moving to the side of the field and interrupting Dom's thoughts as they had tumbled down a rabbit hole.

Shifting his attention back to practice, he lined up behind the center once more.

"Red, thirty-two. Red, thirty-two," he yelled, spotting the middle linebacker approaching the line of scrimmage. In his peripheral vision, he caught the cornerback drifting back. A blitz. Shit. Too late to change the play. "Go! Go!"

The center snapped the ball into Dom's hands. Ronin and Zeph ran their routes, and the offensive line blocked the attacking defensive live. He dropped back, football raised. One step. Two. Three. Four. On the fifth, his gut twisted in a sickening tumble, a too-late warning of something about to go horribly wrong. His plant foot rolled, and he crashed to the ground.

His head slammed to the ground, and a blinding pain burst behind his eyes.

Then his world went black.

...

Oh God.

Jesus.

Panic and terror clawed at Tennyson's throat as she ran up to the University of Washington Medical Center's entrance. Zeph's deep baritone still echoed in her ear from the telephone call that had thrown her world on its ass.

"Tenny, Dom was hurt in practice. He blacked out for a few seconds, so they're taking him to the hospital for tests." Even Zeph's lovely Louisiana drawl hadn't been able to lessen the blow or dial back the terror that had erupted inside her.

Hurt. Blacked out. That's all that had been recycling in her head over and over for the last half hour since she'd received the call and started racing over to the hospital.

A concussion. That's what it had to mean. In the seven years of his career, he'd never suffered this particular injury. This scary, potentially life-changing injury.

"Please, God, let him be okay," she prayed, barely pausing as the glass doors hissed open. "Please—"

The smell hit her first. The strange, unique, but all-too-familiar scent of disinfectant, flowers, detergent, and sickness. Then the sounds infiltrated her senses next. The squeak of soft-soled shoes rushing across a waxed floor. The whispered whine of wheelchairs. The ringing of phones and professionally polite voices under the hum of an ever-circulating AC system. Then the visuals pummeled her. White lab coats. Generic paintings on the wall. Signs with arrows and directions to different departments and areas. People. So many people. Sad people.

Everything—the scents, noises and images—bombarded her, crashed into her like swollen floods released from their gates at one time. The images blurred, melded, overlapped so that for long, suffocating seconds, she wasn't sure if she stood in Seattle or that Dayton hospital so long ago as a child.

Her harsh, shallow breaths wheezed in and out of her lungs, echoing between her ears. Sweat popped out on her forehead, the back of her neck, and prickled under her arms. The world constricted, expanded, then constricted again until it resembled a rubber band.

I can't. I can't do this. The words were a chant inside her head.

But then an image of Dom flickered and solidified behind her lids, momentarily dimming the cacophonous noise, loosening the noose around her throat. Dom, those piercing blue eyes closed. That golden skin, pale; the vitality that seemed to hum off his body, muted.

She swallowed back a humiliatingly childlike whimper and focused on the floor and on putting one foot in front of the other.

"I can do it," she murmured to herself. "I can."

"Tenny?" Ronin's voice penetrated the roar in her head seconds before his fingers wrapped around her upper arm.

Sheer relief and gratefulness flowed through her. Uncaring what he might read into her reaction, she hugged him, a shudder rippling through her.

"Hi," she mumbled against his chest.

"Hey." He returned the embrace, holding her, letting her absorb his strength. Ronin, usually so chatty, didn't utter a word until she inhaled a deep breath and pulled back. "You okay?"

"I really hate hospitals, but yes." She nodded. "Yes, I am."

"Okay, let's go." He wrapped an arm around her shoulders and guided her toward the bank of elevators.

Minutes that felt like a crawling eternity passed, and she had no shame about clinging to Ronin's big, gentle hand. They approached a closed door, and he reached around her and opened it. Voices rushed out to greet her, and she followed them, moving inside.

And there he was.

Her knees weakened, and she propped a shoulder against the wall just inside the doorway. He lay in the hospital bed, still wearing his practice jersey and game pants. An Ace bandage wrapped around his ankle, and the tan material stood out against the stark white sheets. His dark brown hair tumbled around his face, and when he glanced in her direction and she met his blue eyes, she sucked in a breath. His expression might say disgruntled, but his eyes—they revealed his pain and fear.

She pushed off the wall, moving toward him.

"Tenny." He frowned, stretching out a hand toward her, his palm up. "What the hell are you doing here?" Concern darkened the shadows already in his gaze.

She shrugged. "*Paternity Court* was a rerun," she teased, attempting to lighten the heaviness of the conversation. Especially when she was the cause of that concern. He, more than anyone, knew how panic-inducing and traumatic it'd been to walk into this hospital. She clasped his hand in hers, her grip tight.

Dom didn't smile as she'd intended but continued to study her face.

"Oh good, Tenny. You're here," Renee said, flipping her hair over her shoulder and pinning an exasperated but affectionate glare on Dom. "I was five seconds away from running a catheter up in him."

"Kinky," Jason drawled from the other side of the private room.

"Shut it," Renee snapped at her ex. "If I was talking to you, I would've used grunts and single syllables."

"Christ," Ronin muttered.

"What are you guys doing here?" Tennyson interrupted before World War Three could erupt.

"Me and Ronin were at practice already. Renee followed the ambulance here, and I called Jason after talking to you,"

Zeph explained.

"I didn't need an escort," Dom said, his tone more than a little disgruntled.

"I think that's his way of saying thank you for all your help today," Ronin offered, grinning.

"I'm glad you translated for me," Zeph replied. "Because it sounded a lot like he was being an ungrateful douche."

Dom sighed, rolling his head back against the hospital pillow. "Yes, that's exactly what it meant. Hey, can you guys give Tenny and me a minute?"

"Sure." Ronin pushed off the wall and stretched. "Who wants to hit the cafeteria with me? I'm starving."

"I thought you were having dinner with your mother and sisters tonight," Jason reminded him, arching an eyebrow as he headed toward the door.

"It's Natia's birthday," Ronin said, mentioning his youngest sister. He squeezed his eyes closed, pinching the bridge of his nose as if in pain. "I'm going to be surrounded by her and a bunch of seventeen-year-olds. For hours. If not for the league's drug test rules, I'd definitely hit one of Mom's blunts tonight."

Jason snickered, and even though panic hadn't fully removed its teeth, a spurt of humor rose up in her. She'd visited Ronin's home on Vashon Island, where the receiver had grown up with his single mother and four sisters. The farmhouse was loud, boisterous, chaotic, and occasionally smelled of weed. His mother, a beautiful woman of Samoan descent, was a confirmed vegetarian, conspiracy theorist, hippie, and firm believer in smoking marijuana. Although, these days it was medicinal rather than recreational. Ronin loved his family, but visits to the island, which was an hour and fifteen minutes' drive from Seattle, weren't entirely... restful. Or quiet.

She also knew Ronin's mother had recently been

diagnosed with breast cancer. For all his belly-aching, he wouldn't miss time with her or his family for the world. The funny, laid-back wide receiver always had a ready joke or quick comeback. She suspected he covered a lot of his pain with humor. Not that he'd admit it. He was a man, of course.

"I'm just going to head out and hit the road," Ronin said with a sigh. "I guess my stomach can hold," he grumbled. "Call and let me know what the docs say," he ordered Dom before exiting the room.

"I'll check on you later." Zeph directed a chin lift at Dom, then left. Jason and Renee followed, bickering.

Silence permeated the room, the dim sounds of voices and the beeping of machines beyond the closed door low background noise.

The frenetic energy and anxiety that had driven her to the hospital and to his room waned, and she sank down on the bed. Leaning forward, she cupped his face, studying him closely. Noting the weariness, the strain, and glimmers of pain.

"You scared the hell out of me," she murmured. The remnants of that terror still hummed.

For a moment, she thought he would turn his head and press his mouth to her palm like he'd taken to doing this past week. But he didn't; he remained still under her hand, showing no reaction to her touch.

A sliver of icy unease slid through her, freezing her veins.

Dropping her hand to her lap, she tried to ignore the sensation. "Have the doctors taken you for tests yet?"

"Yeah." His mouth firmed, and he glanced away from her. "That's what I'm waiting on now. To hear the results. But I already know what they're going to say. I know my body. It's a sprained ankle and a bump on the head. Not a big deal."

She snorted. "Funny. I don't remember seeing your medical degree on the wall of your house. Besides, you and

I both know the team has a doctor and trainers right there in the facility. If it was 'not a big deal,' they wouldn't have brought you to the hospital."

"I rolled my ankle during practice, fell, hit my head, and blacked out for about twenty seconds. They just want to make sure it's not a concussion. Like I said, not a big deal," he repeated. "The foot, my head—I'll be okay in a few days. Just long enough to miss a game. Just long enough for my backup to replace me on Sunday. *Shit.*" He thrust his fingers through his hair and fisted the strands at the back of his head. Then he released a sharp bark of laughter. "How could I have been so stupid? So careless? My head should've been on practice, on the game. Because it wasn't, I made a dumbass mistake. One that could cost me."

He pressed his thumbs to his eyes, and his harsh breathing reverberated off the cream-colored walls. Her heart ached for him, and if she could, she would've taken his anger, frustration, and hurt onto herself. For him, she would gladly bear it. But she couldn't.

Instead, she laid a hand on his hard thigh. The muscle bunched under her palm. "I know you're upset," she began, softly. "But it could've been worse, and I'm just glad you're okay."

"Could've been worse." He tipped his head back and stared at the ceiling, a bitterness she rarely heard from him coating his words like a dark oil slick. When he lowered his chin and met her gaze, she forced herself to meet the dark swirl of emotion in his blue eyes. "Yeah, it could've been," he continued, a harsh edge to his tone that raked over her skin. "I have a sprained ankle and possibly a concussion because I couldn't keep my head in the game. And now, with my contract up for renewal, I've just handed my backup the opportunity to show his skills and maybe convince the coach and team that he might be a better bet than me." He released another of those humorless, serrated laughs. "So yeah, I'm not so sure about it not being worse."

"Dom…"

"No." He held up a hand. "Tenny, Just… Do you want to know what preoccupied me? What I was thinking about at practice instead of concentrating on the play I was supposed to be running?" He didn't give her an opportunity to answer but barreled on. "You, Tenny. I was so distracted by thoughts of you, of what's going on between us, of you leaving, that I fucked up. I've always been focused, able to block everything out but football. But not yesterday. And it's not the first time I've allowed myself to become so consumed that I'm messing up, losing control." His lips clamped shut, and his jaw clenched, a muscle ticking.

"Just like Tara," she finished for him, hurt leaving her voice hoarse and barely there. "You can say it. You might as well."

But he didn't. Then again, he didn't need to; she heard it as if it'd been announced over the building's PA system.

"I almost lost my scholarship because of her, and that would have fucked up both your life and mine. Damn it, Tenny," he swore, scrubbing his hands down his face. "I don't blame you. This is all my fault. Not yours. This," he waved a hand back and forth between them, "was just the catalyst."

Brian's words slid in her mind, haunting her.

You're a liability.

Let him be great without an albatross weighing him down.

The same panic that had crawled inside her, strangled her when she'd entered the hospital doors, crept in on her now.

"I don't want to be a hindrance to you, to your career," she whispered, her pounding heart in her throat. "But I'm beginning to think in one way or another, I have been…for years."

A heavy silence plummeted between them, her short,

choppy breaths the only sound. *Deny it! Deny it, please!* The scream rebounded off the walls of her skull, deafening her. For a second, she thought she caught a momentary softening of his eyes, his mouth. But in the next instant, a firm, cold resolve hardened his expression.

He didn't reply. Didn't tell her to stop being a drama queen. Didn't utter a sound.

And his awful, heartbreaking quiet was answer enough.

She closed her eyes, returning her hand to her lap and struggling to draw breath into her lungs.

"Tenny..."

She shook her head, hard, eyes still squeezed shut.

"Tenny, look at me." A thin vein of steel threaded through his voice. She wanted to ignore it, refuse him, but in the end, she obeyed. Because she'd never been able to deny him anything. "Why did you come here?"

She blinked. "Wh-what?"

"Why are you here?" he repeated, his blue stare unrelenting, scalpel-sharp. "In this hospital. You braved one of your greatest fears to come here. Why?"

She parted her lips, but no words escaped. A daunting, terrifying thought was dawning on her like an ever-increasing, threatening storm. Where was he going with this?

Oh you know what he means. What he's asking.

"I-I don't know..." she stammered.

His gaze didn't waver, remained penetrating. Knowing. The abyss in her chest yawned wider.

"I always said you were a shitty liar." His hands came down on either side of his legs, and he leaned forward. "You love me."

Shock ricocheted through her. "Of course," she whispered. "You're my friend."

Dom shook his head. "You know what I mean, Tenny. You. Love. Me." Touching her for only the second time since she'd entered the room, he mimicked her caress from earlier and cupped her cheek. "You faced your biggest fear to get to me. Yeah, you love me."

God, if only she didn't. What would it feel like not to love him anymore? Liberating?

Weightless?

Empty. The slick, crafty voice crooned inside her mind.

The truth reverberated inside her, a gong that increased in strength and volume. She could deny her overwhelming love and passion for him to save face. Or she could just admit what he already knew, or had guessed. She could take her heart and her future into her own hands and walk out onto that trembling, thin ledge and risk that he would return her love. Want all of her and not just her body.

Not just her friendship.

"Yes," she whispered. "I do love you. I always have."

"Oh, sweetheart," he breathed.

Her breath caught. Not at the endearment, but the sadness, the *pity* in his eyes. That fucking pity. *Again.*

Pain—agony—surged through her, pouring hot, thick, and heavy. Tears—those damn tears—pricked her eyes. Oh God, not again.

"Tenny." Dom shook his head, his palm still cradling her cheek, still touching her. She couldn't bear it. Jerking her head away, she dislodged his hand and stood from the bed. With deliberate effort, she steadied her weak, shaky knees. "Sweetheart, you're the most important person in my life. But I can't... Damn," he growled, thrusting his fingers through his hair once more. "We were supposed to remain friends."

Her harsh breaths abraded her chest, and the godawful pain continued to tear at her like a ravenous beast with an insatiable appetite. Part of her longed to turn back the clock, not have come to the hospital. Not have said the words that revealed her longest held, deepest secret.

But another part—one she hadn't known existed until that moment—exhaled with relief. That secret had been a burden she'd carried for so long, and with each year that passed, it'd grown heavier, more difficult to bear. Though the humiliation and hurt vibrated within her, the weight of the truth sloughed off her like dead skin. This new skin, it hurt, was sensitive and vulnerable, but at least it meant she was free.

The writers of the Bible had it wrong. It wasn't just the truth that set you free; it was the cold, hard, unforgiving truth that left you without protection or covering and with no other alternative but to face it. And walk in it.

Walk in being the daughter of a woman who'd victimized Tenny because of her own emotional and psychological damage. In being a foster child who never felt like she'd belonged, who struggled to find her identity. In being a woman who loved a man who couldn't—wouldn't—love her as she needed, deserved. In being strong and weak, brave and scared shitless, dependent and hungry for independence.

In being perfectly imperfect.

"You know, for so many years," she said, voice husky with the pain that scraped her throat raw, "I always felt less than when it came to you. Someone as beautiful, talented, gifted, and...perfect as you could never want me when I was none of those things, but the women you dated were all of them."

"Tennyson," he rasped, more of that damn sorrow saturating his voice.

"No." She moved back another step until her back pressed against the wall. She needed to get this said before she couldn't. "I *felt* that way. *Thought* those things. At some point, God, I'm not even sure when, I realized I'm worth love. I deserve it. The kind of love that lights up a man's face when I walk into the room. The kind that movies are written about. The kind that consumes a man so his first thought in the morning is me, and his last word at night is my name. That's the love I want and am worthy of. And I'm finally accepting that you can't give it to me."

She pressed her stacked hands to her chest as if they could contain the storm waging inside her.

"I want to be a man's everything. His number-one priority above all else. For you, football will always come first. And I don't blame you for that, I don't," she assured him, even as part of her mourned it. "Because I know you better than anyone, and I love you more than anyone. I would never ask you to choose between me and your dream. I understand what football means to you. It's so much more than just a game. It's a promise, your stability when the world went to hell. It's the security you've fought for since your parents' death. Believe me, Dom, I get it. But I also know I need more. And for the first time in my life, I'm not going to wait for someone else to make me a priority. I'm going to make myself one. For me. That's the real reason I'm leaving Seattle."

He frowned, and she easily read the confusion and frustration in his expression. "I love you, Tenny. How could you ever doubt that?"

"I know you do. Just not the way I need you to."

"That's not fair," he snapped, but she heard the fear and desperation under the hard, abrupt tone. Recognized it. Because the same emotions rolled and tumbled inside her.

And sadness. As if the end of something loomed near, and she yearned to hold on to it even as she realized she had to let go.

She smiled, feeling her lips tremble with the tears she held back with a will that surprised her. "A fair is a shitfest of carnies and rides. It ain't got fuck-all to do with life," she recited Foster Mom #2's sage advice. And from the pain in his eyes, she assumed he recognized the quote.

Blinking back more tears, she glanced away from him,

shuddering out a breath. "I love you with my whole being—I have since I was sixteen years old—and it's only grown since then," she said, turning back to him. She didn't flinch from the storm in his eyes, his face. "But, I refuse to settle for less than what—who—I need. Not anymore. Goodbye, Dom."

Forcing one foot in front of the other, she exited the room, and fought her way out of the hospital.

All without looking back.

Chapter Fifteen

Dom tipped the bottle of beer to his mouth and took a long pull from it. As the cold alcohol slid over his tongue, he scanned the interior of the packed nightclub from his perch on the VIP leather couch. The cavernous Belltown hot spot boasted three bars with top-shelf liquor, world-renowned DJs, a wide stage, three dance floors, and hundreds of people gyrating to pulsing music that bounced off the three glass walls that separated the main club from the luxurious VIP sections. Though several of his team members partied here often, it was his first time, and if he could help it, his last.

Hell, he didn't want to be here. Contrary to public opinion, this wasn't his scene. Yeah, he didn't mind a night out every now and then, but he didn't drink much during the season. He damn sure didn't dance. And if he wanted female company, he didn't need to come to a meat market like this. But several of his teammates, high off their win over Green Bay, had asked him to come out. Not wanting to rain on their parade, he'd agreed.

No, he hadn't led them to victory tonight—even though

he'd gone through the concussion protocol and had been cleared, and his ankle had felt stable enough for him to play. But Coach and the trainers had disagreed, wanting him to spend another day in the boot. And given the strong showing Jensen had made on the field, Dom's guts had been twisted in knots all afternoon and evening. Still, he was the team's leader until the head office said differently at the end of the season. And since he couldn't be out there with them during the game, he'd decided to celebrate with them here. Free of that damn boot, thank God. He glanced down at his foot. Their team trainer had removed it after the game, and for the first time in days, he felt semi-normal.

Yeah, and even with all that, he'd still rather be home in his favorite sweats, bare feet kicked up on the table, beer in hand, and watching his DVR'd episodes of *Murder Chose Me* and *Homicide Hunter*. He glanced down at his watch. Eleven o'clock. He'd give it another hour before he got ghost.

Sighing, he downed another gulp of his beer, his second of a self-imposed two-beer limit. Temptation to lift that restriction crawled through him like an insidious whisper. What did it matter? And at least for a night, he could forget about all the crap that had rained down on him in the last few days. His injuries at practice. Missing an important game. Jensen.

Tenny.

His fingers tightened around the bottle, and he clenched his jaw, bracing himself against the slash of pain and betrayal that tore at him. Yeah, he wouldn't mind not thinking about how, according to Zeph, she'd left for Dayton the day before, how she would be moving thousands of miles away from home. From him.

And wasn't that what hurt like a bitch?

No, what hurt more was watching her walk away after he'd told her she was a hindrance to his career. He might not have uttered the words, but his silence had made his agreement with her statement clear.

Fuck.

He tilted the bottle up for another long, deep pull. As if the alcohol could wash away the memory of her face, her brokenness as he crushed her with his silence and his rejection of her love.

He'd been…frozen. Fear and panic had gripped every one of his senses, organs, and limbs, holding him hostage. How could he have explained to her that, with her, he'd done what he'd vowed he never would again? After the spectacular clusterfuck that had been his relationship with Tara, he hadn't felt that powerless or helpless since his parents died. His feelings for her had clouded every aspect of his life, threatening the future he'd pursued for his father, for himself…for Tenny. He'd promised himself he would never, ever allow another relationship to influence his career. To distract him from the game that not only had defined him for so many years, but *saved* him.

Despite his best, most vigilant intentions, he'd failed with Tenny. First, the date that Brian had arranged. Then being distracted in practice. Then becoming injured. He'd broken his own rule. And that couldn't happen. It was a slippery slope. And at the feet of the slope would be the shattered remains of his career as well as the most important friendship in his life.

And though he sat on this leather couch in a club's VIP section, that's where he actually stood—at the feet of that slope.

I do love you. I always have.

He didn't need her love, damn it. The fingers pulsed in protest at his tight hold on the bottle. Love meant one thing: getting seriously fucked over.

And Tennyson had proved it by walking away from him.

From all they'd meant to each other for fourteen years. After his parents died, he'd only allowed people so close. Those in his life—foster parents, his adopted parents, his teammates—could be gone at any time due to moves, too many kids, college, or trades. Even with Zeph and Ronin, though they were his best friends, just the nature of their careers could mean one day they wouldn't be in the same locker room or city. So while he'd let them further in than most others, Dom still erected a protective wall around himself. Only Tenny had been permitted to enter that place guarded by emotional barbed wire. He hadn't even allowed Tara inside the places Tenny inhabited.

Now, she was abandoning him.

Just like the two people you loved most.

He shook his head hard, as if the abrupt motion could jar loose the traitorous thought. What the hell? He was too damn old to play the blame game. The twelve-year-old boy might've been angry at them for leaving, but the man understood they wouldn't have if they'd been offered the choice.

Unlike Tenny. Who'd not only made the decision but had sought the opportunity to move several states away. How ironic that he'd been worried that sex would damage their relationship, when it'd been in trouble even before the first time they'd made love.

Made love. As soon as the phrase echoed in his head, he mentally recoiled from it. He didn't make love; he fucked. One required commitment, promises. The other just good ol' fashioned animal lust. That's what he did...what he'd always do.

Even the words rang hollow in his head.

The truth was his best friend had left a wide, gaping hole in his life, in his fucking chest, since she'd walked out of that hospital room three days ago.

"For someone who's supposed to be celebrating, you

look like someone pissed in your cornflakes," Ronin said, dropping onto the couch next to him. Leaning forward, he nabbed one of the bottles from the ice bucket on the low table in front of them. "I was wondering why you agreed to come out. This isn't really your thing."

Dom didn't immediately reply, instead chugging another gulp of beer. "I could say the same for you," he finally said, arching an eyebrow. "How did you get in here wearing that anyway? Doesn't this place have a dress code?"

Ronin glanced down at his black T-shirt with a vintage Harley Davidson logo, worn, ripped jeans, and brown hiking boots. "What's wrong with what I have on? This is my best shirt."

Snorting, Dom shook his head.

"You know just because Jensen had one good game doesn't mean he's going to replace you, right? The kid's good, but he's still young and needs more experience. And besides, you're our quarterback. There's not a man on this team who doesn't recognize that or doesn't have your back." The observation, as well as Ronin's uncharacteristically serious tone, had Dom jerking his head in his friend's direction. "You think I don't know what's being bothering you? What's been bothering you since Wednesday?" Ronin continued, giving Dom a mocking half smile. He tapped his temple with the opening of his bottle. "Vulcan mind meld. You bitches better not ever doubt me again." He grinned, his gravity disappearing as if it'd never been.

Dom stared at his friend, unable to speak because of the boulder of emotion lodged in his throat. He sipped his beer, nodding at Ronin. And maybe the other man understood, because he clapped him on the shoulder, then turned and started flirting with their cocktail waitress.

"Dom!" the familiar voice called out his name, and Dom glanced in the direction of the entrance to the VIP section.

Brian stood in the door, partially blocked by the club's security.

Frowning, Dom jerked his chin at the built-like-a-tank bouncer, indicating he could allow his agent in the cordoned-off area. The man shifted aside, and Brian entered, followed by a tall, slender, lovely redhead in a short, tight, black dress that showcased all her...assets.

"Daaaaaamn." Ronin drawled. "That Brian's woman?"

"I don't know," Dom said, shrugging. "She looks familiar, though."

"Dom, Ronin." Brian approached them with a big grin. He settled a palm on the small of the woman's back as Ronin and Dom stood. "I'd like you both to meet Megan Wright. Megan, Dominic Anderson and Ronin Palamo, quarterback and wide receiver for the Washington Warriors."

"Nice to meet you, Megan," Ronin greeted with a smile.

"Megan." Dom extended his hand, and she slid her palm across his. "A pleasure."

Her fingers squeezed his, holding on a couple of seconds longer than the required, polite handshake. *O-kay.* Dom glanced at Brian, but his agent seemed oblivious to his date's flirting. Extricating his hand, he switched his attention to Brian. "When I talked to you earlier, you didn't mention coming here."

Brian's smile widened. "It was a spur of the moment decision. I was having dinner with Megan and her agent when we spoke. Since she's been wanting to meet you, we swung by."

"Megan's agent?" Dom repeated, suspicion burrowing inside him.

"Yes. Since you were unable to attend her movie premiere, I thought this would be a wonderful opportunity for you two to finally get together." Brian shifted his hold to Megan's elbow and guided her down to the cushion next to

Dom. "She's a huge fan."

"I am." Megan smiled, settling close beside him, her blue eyes warm with an invitation he had no intention of accepting. He wasn't being narcissistic; he'd been around and with enough women to recognize when one was attracted to him and throwing signals. Megan was hurling them at a hundred miles an hour. "Last year, you passed for fifty touchdowns during the regular season, three game-winning drives, a 75% completion percentage, and a 99.9 quarterback rating."

He blinked. "Okay, I believe you're a fan," he drawled, even as anger slid through his veins. Fucking Brian had ambushed him after he'd told the bastard he had no intention of meeting or hooking up with the actress. What? Had he believed seeing her face-to-face and finding out she could recite stats would change his mind?

"I hope you don't mind us barging in on your night. Since you couldn't make the premiere, which I was really disappointed about," she purred, wearing a pout that, at one time, he might have found sexy, "I jumped on this chance." Her fingers gently touched his thigh, and he barely managed to control the flinch from her touch. It felt…wrong.

"Megan, I'm hoping you might be able to change his mind now that he's met you," Brian said with a chuckle.

His agent's remark struck a match to the fury already pouring through him. Dom struggled to hang on to his polite smile, when he really longed to shove her hand off him and punch his agent in the face for putting him in this position.

"Listen, Megan, I'm sorry." Dom stood, hoping his smile didn't appear as fake as it felt on his mouth. Well, actually, nope. He didn't give a flying fuck if it did. "Brian, can I speak with you for a moment? Privately," he stressed, injecting enough steel into the request his agent would have to be deaf not to recognize it as a demand.

Not waiting to hear or receive Brian's agreement, Dom

strode from the VIP section. He descended the steps and waited for the other man in the alcove beneath the staircase. Seconds later, his agent appeared.

"What the fuck, Brian?" he growled.

"What?" Brian shrugged, his palms held face up. "What's the problem?"

"Don't play dumb. It's not a good look," Dom snapped. "And it's an insult. What the hell were you thinking bringing Megan Wright here after I told you I didn't want to be seen with her?"

"No," Brian disagreed, cocking his head to the side. "You said you didn't want to escort her to the premiere. You didn't mention anything about not being seen with her."

"So we're splitting hairs now?" He laughed, and he wasn't in the least bit amused. He was pissed. "You know damn well what I meant. I said no, but you're just going to force me to bend to what you want? I thought I was the client and had the final say."

His agent's mouth twisted into a sneer. "C'mon, Dom. We both know you made that decision with your dick."

"Excuse me?" A flicker of anger leaped in his chest, burning there and growing hotter by the second.

Brian scoffed. "What? You didn't think I wouldn't notice? Wouldn't know that you and your *best friend* are fucking?" His sneer deepened into something uglier. "Admit it, Dom. You wouldn't have turned down this opportunity if not for her. I told her she was a hindrance to you. Dead weight. An albatross that's been dragging you down from the beginning. It's time you made a decision about what's more important to you. A chick or your future."

Dead weight. Dragging you down.

A hindrance.

Immediately, Tenny's statement punched him in the gut.

"I don't want to be a hindrance to you, to your career."

That flicker burst into a backdraft of fury. It'd been Brian who'd put that shit in Tenny's head. Brian who had made her feel like a detriment to Dom's career. Brian who'd—

No, that was you, asshole, the snide indictment from inside his head taunted.

He smothered an anguished moan.

Brian might've planted the seeds of that thought, but it'd been Dom who'd sown and nurtured it with his actions and complicit silence. And all because he'd been too afraid of losing control over his career, his life... So instead, he'd been a coward and driven her away.

She'd never been a stumbling block, a *hindrance*. At one point, her very existence had pushed him to keep his head on straight when he could've easily tripped off that path into drugs or crime. As angry as he'd been, even in spite of being adopted and given a family, that decision might not have surprised anyone. But because of Tennyson, because she'd needed him, he'd played his ass off and worked hard so they could both have lives they'd only dreamed about. She'd been his anchor, his one security, because when everything changed around him, she never had.

If not for her, he may not have had football, his career, his present or future.

So now he had to decide. Did he exist in fear, constantly protecting himself? Or did he live how he ran out on that football field every Sunday? Bold, resilient, unafraid, confident that he didn't have to guard himself because he had someone—Tennyson—who cared about him already doing so.

So yes, *God yes*.

He had nothing without her. His game sucked. His playing sucked. His fucking life sucked.

He chose her.

A rush of breath exhaled from his lungs. Hope and a fair

share of fear huddled in his chest.

Fear of moving out of their friendship that was as familiar and comfortable to him as running out on that field every day. Fear of fumbling and ruining the most important relationship in his life. Fear of not knowing what the fuck he was doing.

But he had to try.

He clapped Brian on the shoulder. "Thank you, Brian."

The other man frowned, but then grinned, a smug satisfaction suffusing his expression. "Of course. You're welcome. That's what I'm here for, to help you make the tough decisions."

"You're so right." Dom pounded Brian on the shoulder again. "By the way, you're fired."

Striding away while his ex-agent sputtered in outrage, Dom pulled his phone from the inside pocket of his jacket. He scrolled through his contacts and located the number he needed. After hitting call, he listened to the other line ring several times as he maneuvered through the throngs of people.

"Declan." Though the game had been over for hours and he should've been home, relaxing, Coach Declan sounded alert and wide awake. Knowing the man, he was probably back at his office in the practice facility. He never stopped working.

"Hey, Coach," Dom greeted, more of that fear throbbing inside him. "I need to meet with you tomorrow. The earlier the better."

"You've called me now, Dom. Talk. What's the problem? If it's about whether or not you're playing in the upcoming game, you know I won't make that decision until Friday," his coach warned.

Pushing through a side exit, Dom cupped the back of his neck, staring down at the ground. "It's not about that. Well, in a way it is. God." He blew out a hard breath. These were the hardest words he'd ever had to say to this man. "Coach, I'm going to miss practice on Wednesday and Thursday." If not for an appointment on Tuesday that had been arranged weeks ago—an appointment he needed to keep—he would leave tonight.

A long pause seemed to echo louder and louder over the line.

"Excuse me?" the other man said, softly. Ominously.

Damn. Even as he uttered the words, he still couldn't believe he'd stated them. He was about to commit a mortal football sin, very possibly lose his chance to play Sunday or any games after that. Hell, he was about to put everything on the line.

But for Tenny, it was worth it.

"If it wasn't important, there's no way in hell I'd miss a practice, but trust me, Coach. It's important," he said, knowing that excuse wasn't going to fly with the stern but fair man.

"I'm not going to sugarcoat shit for you, Dom." Dom caught the creak as if the other man was adjusting his large frame in his ancient office chair. "A fine is the least of your worries when it comes to skipping out. You've been injured, you didn't play this week, and we won. Add in you haven't been at your best the last few games. Your position could be on the line for the rest of the season. And it could mean your damn job with your contract up for renewal. Is what you're missing practice for worth all that?"

Dom sighed, everything Coach Declan pointed out piling up like bricks on his shoulders. This was what he'd worked for, to not just play, but to start for the Warriors. To be the best. Now, as he faced the possibility of watching all he'd worked so hard for slip between his fingers, none of it terrified him as much as losing Tenny forever. Of not having her in his life.

"Yes," he answered Declan's question. "Yes, it's worth it. I know I'm in somewhat of a slump. But if I don't somehow fix what I'm missing practice for, that slump won't be fixed either."

He didn't know how seeing Tenny would solve his issues with his season and his playing, but one thing was as certain and strong for him as the stench of piss in the side alley he stood in.

If he didn't talk to her, make a play for her, tell her how much of an asshole he'd been, his game would just get worse. And so would his life.

A heavy sigh rolled down the connection. "Fine, Dom. If your mind is made up, there's nothing I can say. But just know nothing is guaranteed, and there are consequences for everything."

As Dom said goodbye and ended the call, Coach Declan's last words reverberated in his head like an eerie foreshadowing.

He was headed to Dayton, but he had no idea what awaited him when he got there.

Chapter Sixteen

Tennyson emerged from the hotel bathroom, the steam from her shower following her out. Sighing, she tightened the belt of her robe around her and pulled the band from her hair.

God, she was tired.

She glanced at the digital clock over her shoulder on the bedside table. Just two o'clock in the afternoon. But it might as well have been two a.m. considering the weariness that weighed down her shoulders like wet sandbags.

Unable to sleep the night before, she'd stared at the cream-colored walls of her hotel room for hours. Nerves hadn't kept her up; she'd like to blame her tossing and turning on anxiety and excitement over this job opportunity—this possible new life—for her. But she couldn't.

The past few weeks had sped through her mind like a movie reel. Moments of joy, laughter, desire, anger, disappointment, and grief. Images of Zeph, Ronin, Sophia, Renee...Dom. Always Dom. Especially those last moments in the hospital room.

When the infomercials finally started to roll on, she'd

gratefully dropped off in a restless doze. Because her mind had slowed down, the memories had paused even for those few, short hours.

An extra layer of makeup had been required that morning so she didn't resemble the walking dead for her eleven o'clock interview at the County offices. An interview that she'd managed to reschedule to Wednesday since she was in Dayton a week early. It had gone very well. Better than she could've hoped.

And a part of her still remained shell-shocked that she'd turned the job down.

Exhaling, she flattened her palms on the bathroom counter and leaned forward, studying her reflection. Exhaustion stared back at her. Hurt did as well. Even a little bit of fear. But so did strength and resolve. Certainty.

At some point between the fountain of youth miracle cream infomercial and an episode of *Law & Order: Criminal Intent*, she'd had an epiphany. All of this—her secret of unrequited love, keeping Dom in the dark for years about her feelings, refusing to tell Dom she loved him—had been more about her than Dom. *Her* insecurities, *her* doubts, *her* fears.

She'd started this journey to Dayton, had pursued it, because it'd meant finally discovering who Tennyson Clark was meant to be. Finding out if she could stand on her own without Dom as a safety net. Learning to forge her own path, be her own person. Those had been her reasons for moving to Dayton. At least the ones she'd told herself to justify the truth.

She was running. From her past. From her feelings for Dom. From herself.

And, God, she was so tired of running.

On Monday and Tuesday, she'd spent hours scoping out possible apartments, but she'd also visited the house she'd lived in with her mother. It was abandoned now, the windows boarded up, the steps cracked and broken, her one parent long gone. But standing on that sidewalk, remembering the terrified child she'd been, it'd hit her: she was a survivor. She'd not just endured, but *survived*.

The strength she'd been seeking in herself had been there all along.

That sounded cheesy as hell even in her own head, but there it was.

So she was going home. To Seattle. Back to her family, the one she'd created through close friendships rather than birth. Back to her present *and* her future. And if it didn't include Dom, okay. She could deal with that. Because none of what she'd told him last Thursday had changed. She deserved someone who loved her above everything else. The house of her childhood had only reaffirmed that resolve.

She wasn't returning to Seattle for him, but for her.

A quick, hard knock echoed in the hotel room.

For several seconds, she frowned, staring at the door. Who could that possibly be? She hadn't ordered room service. And it was extremely doubtful Veronica Maitland had showed up to ask her to reconsider. She snorted. Yeah, right.

Still frowning, she crossed the room and pressed her eye to the peephole.

Oh my God. It couldn't...

Heart thumping against her sternum like a jackhammer, she peered once more through the glass. But the person on the other side remained the same.

Dom.

She blinked. Blinked again, making no move to open the door.

A low drone buzzed in her ears. Mouth dry, she tried to swallow, but couldn't. He hadn't reached out to her once in the six days since she'd walked out of his hospital room. What was he doing here? And why now? What did he want?

The firm rap of a fist sounded again.

You can do this. So seeing him again was happening sooner than she'd expected. It didn't change anything between them. Didn't change that she'd decided to move on.

Inhaling a deep breath, she straightened her shoulders, lifted her chin, and opened the door.

Her grip on the knob tightened, and for several precious seconds she swore it was the only thing that held her up, kept her grounded. Prevented her from being sucked into the vortex that was Dom.

God, he was…beautiful.

This strong, powerful man who stared at her with such bright, hot intensity it sizzled over skin. Years of habit almost had her moving forward to hug him, but at the last moment, she checked herself. They were no longer "Dom and Tenny." She was no longer that girl-turned-woman whose world revolved around him, hoping that one day he would really see her, love her as she needed.

Now she loved her own self.

"Dom," she said, proud that her voice didn't tremble or sound weak.

"Hey, Tenny." Silence fell between them as they continued to stare at each other on opposite sides of the threshold. Finally, slipping his hands in the front pockets of his pants, he dipped his head in the direction of the room behind her. "Can I come in?"

No, self-preservation roared. But she still stepped to the side and waved him inside. She closed the door behind them, and for an instant, she leaned against it, still stunned that he stood here. In Dayton. With her.

"What are you doing here?" she asked, her voice a hell of a lot stronger than her knees at the moment. "It's Wednesday. You should be at practice."

He nodded. "Yeah, and I'm going to be fined heavily

for missing practice, and no doubt benched for this coming game. Maybe games, according to Coach." He lifted an arm, as if reaching for her, but she stiffened. A flicker of emotion spasmed across his face, and he lowered his hand, sliding it back into his pocket. "I needed to talk to you."

She pushed off the door, crossing her arms over her chest. "I thought we covered everything in the hospital. I don't think there's anything left to say."

He glanced away from her, his throat working. When he returned his gaze to her, she couldn't decipher the shadows darkening his blue eyes. "I know you have your plans here in Dayton, and I swear I'm not going to try and change your mind. Just…give me a few minutes, okay?"

Again, that instinct to protect herself objected. But she nodded.

"First—and I need you to listen to this carefully and accept it—you could never be a burden to me. I know I fucked up and didn't say the right words in the hospital… Hell, didn't say anything. And I'm sorry for that. I'm sorry I hurt you, Tenny. But please believe that I depend on you just as much as you've leaned on me. If not more. I know Brian put that hindrance bullshit into your head, and I'm pleading with you to take it back there, dump it, and light the bitch on fire. You could never weigh me down. Just the opposite. You lift me up." He trapped her in his bright gaze, the power of it startling in its intensity. "Tell me you understand that, sweetheart."

"Don't call me that," she said. Though she sounded firm, even a little cold, inside she quaked at the endearment. She couldn't bear to hear him use the name he'd whispered to her time and again while they made love—correction. Fucked. It blistered her heart like acid poured on an emotional wound.

His eyes briefly closed, and his lips moved as he uttered something too low for her to catch. But when his lashes lifted, more than a little pain gleamed there. Like moments earlier when she first opened the door, she almost reached out to him, but again, she stopped herself.

"I'm an idiot," he murmured, his tone almost subdued. As if he were talking aloud to himself rather than her. "For so long I didn't see, truly see, your beauty. Of course, I knew you were lovely, but I didn't see the wild fire of your hair. The pretty darkness of your eyes. Your sexy, wide mouth. The proud elegance of your features. The curves of a body that was created to take, welcome, and love a man. I don't understand how I missed what was right under my nose for so long, but that's my sin, not yours. While I've been an ass, you've always been...you. And I've missed you." Removing his hands from his pockets, he shifted forward, erasing some of the space between them. "God, I've missed you." He shook his head, and a small frown creased his forehead. "Not just touching you, tasting you, sliding deep inside you. Yeah, all of that, but so much more. I've missed coming home, finding you in the kitchen, and inhaling the delicious scents of what you've cooked. Missed sitting on the couch and watching movies with you. Missed talking to you, seeing you...just being with you. I didn't realize how empty my life was until you weren't there."

What she wouldn't have given to hear this declaration just a week ago. Now...

"What are you saying, Dom? What do you want from me?" She lowered her arms, holding her hands out, palms up. "I can't go back to how we were. Everything was good for you, but for me? I lived a half-life where I couldn't be honest with the most important person in my life because I feared rejection, of losing our friendship. I don't want to live that lie again. I won't."

"I'm not asking you to, Tenny," he said, his gaze intense, piercing.

She glanced away from it. But, in the next second,

returned it. No more ducking, no more dodging. She'd found her voice in the last week; she would use it.

"I don't know if I could trust you, Dom," she admitted, her voice cracking just a little on the confession, reflecting the fissures zigzagging across her heart. She caught his flinch, and a part of her hurt for causing him pain. But she couldn't take back the truth. She'd been doing that for far too long. "With my safety, my physical well-being and security, yes. There's no other person who could protect me, provide for me, care for me. But trust you with my heart?" She pressed her palm to her chest. "I don't know if I want to risk that again."

A week away hadn't diminished her love and need for him. Hell, maybe nothing would. But he'd broken her heart in that hospital room. He'd left her emotionally bruised. She'd laid herself in front of him, bared herself, made herself completely vulnerable. And he'd betrayed it. No. She curled her fingers, as if she could squeeze her pounding heart and make it stop beating. Stop aching. She'd braved the fire of Dom's rejection and came out stronger for it. But opening herself to him again… She was afraid to chance it.

"Tennyson," he whispered, her name a husky rasp full of so much….what? Pain? Sadness? Fear? Frustration? Or maybe that was her just projecting her emotions on him. "The ride to the airport, during the flight, and on the drive here, I had no clue what to say. Just that I had to speak with you. To apologize. To convince you how important you are to me. Tell you how much I need you. And that's all true. But…" He thrust his fingers through his hair, his strong, rigid jaw clenching, a muscle ticking along it. "But," he repeated, voice rougher, hoarser. "Standing here, looking at you, seeing for myself how I've fucked up so bad, I feel you slipping away from me, and I can't do shit about it. I feel like I'm fighting for my life, and I'm losing."

His blue eyes burned into hers. Slowly, he spread his arms

wide, as if offering himself to her. Wide open. Vulnerable.

"You've been my reason for never giving up. Now you're my reason for breathing," he rasped. "Not football. Not my parents. Not the team. Not a championship trophy. But you. It's always been you. Has been for a long time, only I was too blind and dumb to see it."

He paused, swallowed hard, lowering his arms. "If anyone had asked me a week ago if I wanted a relationship, possibly a family, I would've said no. More people to lose to the whims of fate or God or whatever? No, hell no. But fourteen years ago, it'd already been too late. The decision had been made for me. A girl with large, dark eyes had burrowed her way into my heart and set up residence in it. And years later, the woman had claimed it for her own. I want to share my life with you. I want to have the family that was stolen from me with you."

Her breath turned jagged in her lungs. She claimed his heart? A relationship? A family? *Oh God*. The part of her that never stopped hoping, never stopped dreaming, leaped for joy. But the other part—the one that had been rejected by him before, that had been slapped down and disappointed too many times—warned her to proceed with caution. To stop his flow of words before she weakened and gave in.

She squeezed her eyes shut, the battle between her head and heart raging strong.

"Look at me, Tenny. Please." Unable to resist him, she obeyed. And noted the stark lines of strain bracketing his mouth. Saw the pain in the blue depths of his eyes. Caught the uncertainty in his voice. The…desperation. "You have no reason to trust me. And I only have myself to blame. But there's one more thing I need you to hear. If I'm lucky, I'll have a long career. And by 'long' I mean maybe seven or eight more years. But when it's over? What will I have? Who will be there to share my life? To give me a family, a reason for all of the years spent on the field? To affirm that I'm more than a fast body and stats? Without you, Tenny, none of this is worth having."

Shifting back a step, he removed his phone from his pocket. His fingers swept over the screen before he extended the cell toward her. "Here."

Confused, she accepted it, glancing down to see a link.

Drawing in a shaky breath, she clicked on it, and a video started to play.

Dom and a man she recognized as one of ESPN's journalists filled the phone screen. Of course. She'd scheduled the interview—an *Outside the Lines* type piece—several weeks ago. The anchor introduced Dom as the All-Star quarterback of the Washington Warriors. A montage of pictures of Dom's football career, from high school, to college, and finally to the league played along with a narration of his stats and successes.

They mentioned the death of his parents and being adopted by his high school coach, along with how he'd persevered to become one of the top picks in the draft his senior year at Ohio State. The commentator relayed his career with the Warriors, before the camera shifted to a studio shot of Dom and the ESPN journalist. After several questions about his season and the game, the topic switched to the personal aspect the show was known for.

"One of the things most often mentioned about you is your mental toughness," the host said. "What do you attribute this focus and strength to?"

Dom propped his elbows on the arms of the chair and steepled his fingers under his chin. "I think it's common knowledge that my parents passed away in a car accident when I was twelve years old. I spent a couple of years in the foster care system before I was adopted by my coach. Most people would assume that could account for my focus and perseverance. But they would be wrong. I attribute it to one person who gave me a reason to push forward when I could've easily gone down a different, more destructive path."

"A person?" the host repeated.

Dom nodded. "What *isn't* common knowledge is that I met my best friend in foster care. She became my rock. Anytime I thought about playing hooky, skipping practice, hanging out in places I had no business being, I remembered she was counting on me. And at that time, I needed to be needed. I'd lost my parents, my security, my stability. She gave that to me; she offered me purpose, a reason to succeed, to be the best. To get into the league so we could both have a future. I guess some people could look at it and think I saved her. But the truth is, she saved me."

The journalist blinked, appearing momentarily stunned. She sympathized with him. Her breath lodged in her throat, shock paralyzing her. *But the truth is, she saved me.* The words, as well as the passion in his voice, resonated in her, causing tears to sting her eyes.

"I'm curious," the other man said, recovering. "Are you still friends today?"

"Of course," Dom replied. "You don't let people that important leave your life."

The interview continued, and the anchor brought up Dom's recent injury. "Just a couple of weeks ago, you suffered a head injury in practice. You were cleared for a concussion, but you did have a sprained ankle. You ended up not being able to play against Green Bay because of it. That must've been difficult for you."

"That's an understatement." Dom chuckled. "There's competitive, and then there's me," he drawled, and the anchor laughed at the self-deprecating remark.

"Did the injury start you thinking about the mortality of your career? About how long you would continue and what life holds for you after football?"

"Definitely." Dom paused, folding his hands on his lap and studying them for a moment as if gathering his thoughts. "Especially the possible concussion. Thank God I was cleared, but I was reminded that when this part of my life ends, I want to be able to look back and say football was what I did, not who I am. I want to be a husband, a father, a blessing in someone else's life. Do I want to be known as one of the greatest quarterbacks in the game? Of course. I would be a liar if I said it didn't matter. But I realized it's not the most important thing."

"What is the most important thing to you?" the host pressed.

"Tennyson Clark."

Oh my God. Tennyson pressed a fist to her chest, certain her heart would burst through at any second. Jesus, had she heard him correctly? No. She couldn't have. He wouldn't have said something like that on a nationally televised interview. Who did that? Not Dom. Not Mr. Football. She clutched the phone so tight the case poked her fingers.

"A name." The anchor smiled wide, probably sensing he was being handed one of the most sensational interviews of the season. "Would this by any chance be the name of your childhood best friend?"

"Yes," Dom affirmed with a quirk to the corner of his mouth. "That's her. My best friend. And the woman I hope can forgive me for being blind for so long to how much I love her."

"Is this your way of groveling?" the other man teased.

"No, my way of groveling is telling her that if she decides to move back to Dayton, I'll follow her," Dom stated.

The pressure against her sternum swelled so huge, she couldn't contain it. The pain, the grief, the loneliness—it escaped her on a thick, hard sob.

The anchor cocked his head, his eyebrows arched high. "Are you saying you would leave Washington?"

"I love the Warriors—my team, my friends, my coaches, the city. They welcomed me, offered me a place to play as well as call home. I consider my teammates my family, and to finish out my career as a Warrior would be my first choice. But since we were younger, Tennyson has supported my dreams, my passion, and now I'll do whatever's in my power to support her. So yes, that's a discussion we would need to have, because while I love football, she's my life."

"Not many men would have the courage to admit that," the anchor said, leaning forward and extending his hand to Dom. "Thank you for sharing it."

He wrapped up the interview, and when the video ended and the screen went black, she continued to stare at it. What had just happened? Had he just declared he would leave the Warriors for her? Oh Christ.

Stunned, she raised her stare from the phone to him.

This time, when he stretched his arm toward her, she didn't pull back. He tunneled his fingers into the hair above her ear, fisting the strands. A shudder rippled through his big body, and he exhaled, slow, deep.

"Tenny," he whispered, voice thick, heavy with emotion. "I meant every word in that interview. I'm sorry it took this long for someone—*for me*—to tell you how extraordinary, and special, and beautiful you are. Never again will you have to go without hearing it. If you'll let me...if you'll forgive me...I'll make it my purpose in life to remind you every day." He burrowed the fingers of his other hand in her hair, too, so he cradled her head between his palms. "I let you walk away from me once, but never again. I'm following. Wherever you walk or run, I'm going to be right behind you, convincing you of my faithfulness and love until you either get tired of running or start believing."

Releasing her, he again moved back, placing space between them. But his gaze... It was her turn to shiver. Because that gaze didn't release her at all. Just the opposite; it entrapped her. Refused to let go.

"I love you," he said. His declaration surged through her, swelling, crashing like a massive wave. She'd heard those three words before, but never with the passion, the need, the reverence that echoed in them now. The same passion, need, and reverence that flowed through her, drowning her.

"Say it again," she breathed.

His face twisted as if in pain, but it was relief she glimpsed in the gleam of his eyes, the softness of his mouth. Relief and joy.

"I love you," he repeated, cupping her cheeks and pressing his forehead to hers. "Sweetheart, so much."

Sweetheart. Before, she'd ordered him not to call her that. This time, she treasured it.

"I believe you," she murmured. Tears pricking her eyes, she encircled his wrists, rose on her toes, and brushed her mouth over his. "And I love you, too."

"Damn, I was afraid I'd never hear you say that to me again. I'm never going to get tired of hearing it." He captured her mouth again, his tongue thrusting between her lips, tasting her, claiming her. And she claimed him right back. "Tell me again."

"I love you, Dom," she whispered, and opened her lips wider, offering him more of her. Knowing he wouldn't reject her, but would cherish not just her body, but her heart.

Breaking the kiss, she threw her arms around his neck, tipped her head back and laughed. Oh God, it felt good to do that.

She shook her head. "Damn, I'm just flabbergasted."

He grinned. "You're using one of your ten-dollar words, so I'll take that as a good sign."

"The video," she rasped, still more than a little shocked over it. "It was…"

"Over the top?" He smoothed a hand over her hair, then trailed the backs of his fingers along her jaw. "I know. Greg said it will either piss the head office off or have them scrambling to keep me since they're on notice that I'm willing to leave."

She shook her head. "Greg?"

"My new agent," he clarified, his smile now containing a hard edge. "I fired Brian's ass. He admitted the shit he said to you, and I got rid of him on the spot."

He kicked Brian to the curb for her? These revelations were going to do her in. Those tears that had stung her eyes spilled over. "Damn it," she muttered. "No one has ever…" Her throat closed, and she was unable to finish the sentence.

"Shh." He swept his fingers over her damp cheeks. "I would do that and more. You're my world."

"Thank you." She kissed him, pouring into the mating of mouths everything she couldn't say. "Now," she brushed her lips over his chin, "take me home."

Surprise and joy flared in his eyes. "What about the interview? The job?"

"You've given me a family, a home, a place to belong." She brushed her fingertips over his jaw, his mouth, his eyebrows. She just couldn't stop touching him. "All of those are in Seattle. I've already turned the position down and was heading home when you showed up."

"Tenny," he rasped against her hair, pulling her back into a tight embrace. "I wouldn't have asked you to do that. You didn't have to."

"I know," she said. "And I have a couple of conditions."

Threading his fingers through her hair, he scattered kisses over her cheeks and mouth. "Anything you want."

"First, you pick my replacement from that stack of

résumés because I really am quitting as your PA."

He laughed. "Done. What else?"

"I'm setting up an appointment with a counselor because I'm getting over this fear of hospitals. That needs to be in my past where it belongs. I need you to not let me chicken out."

His gaze roamed her face, and she flushed from the admiration he didn't try to hide. "Done. And I know you can do it. The way you barreled into that hospital room? You'll conquer it," he murmured. "What else?"

She pressed her lips to his chest, cherishing every strong beat of his heart. A heart that she no longer doubted belonged solely to her.

"Get me naked."

Dom grinned, and bending, cupped her ass and hiked her in the air. Laughing, she wrapped her arms and legs around him as he headed toward the bed. Seconds later, she bounced against the mattress, and his big body came down, covering her.

"Done."

Epilogue

When the security alarm beeped and the front door to their house—*holy shit,* their *house*—opened, Tennyson stood in the foyer, waiting for Dom while wearing his jersey. And nothing else. Except maybe a wide grin.

Dom punched in the code to silence the alarm and turned. Then froze. His duffel bag hit the floor with a thud, and heat flared in his blue, hooded eyes. His gaze traveled from the top of her head, down her unbound breasts beneath the jersey that barely covered her girly parts, and continued to her bare feet. On the slow return trip, he lingered over her upper thighs, and her flesh started to tingle and pulse in response. Yep, he could still turn her completely on with just one look. The man had skills.

"Congratulations," she greeted, straightening her arms from behind her back and revealing the two bottles of Corona she'd hidden. "You were awesome."

She grinned, and his beautiful mouth turned up in an answering smile. Despite missing Wednesday and Thursday's practices to come declare his undying love in Ohio, his coach had played Dom. After a dismal first half with the backup quarterback, where the Warriors lagged behind the division leading Carolina Panthers at 28 to 7, Coach Declan had put Dom in. And her man had shown the fuck out. The Warriors had pulled out the win against the Panthers, 35 to 28, final score. All of the commentators were off their heads over the fact that number seven had his mojo back.

"Thanks, sweetheart," he said, peeling off his coat and dropping it to the floor alongside his bag. He removed his sneakers and left those there, too. "Which is my present? The beer or you?"

"Why choose?" she asked, twisting off the cap and, tipping her head back, downing a large, long gulp. "I was reading up on things we could do with beer that didn't sound all that sanitary but hella fun." She twirled the bottle by the neck, chuckling when he stalked forward, dragging his thermal shirt over his head.

God, she'd never imagined she could be this happy. It'd only been three days since they'd returned from Dayton, but her world had shifted, changed so it was almost unrecognizable. She'd applied to DSHS Children's Administration for a social worker position. In the meantime, she'd also narrowed down two candidates to replace her as Dom's PA, and he hadn't vetoed either one. And, her first appointment with a counselor was set for the following Wednesday. Yes, she'd been super busy.

She'd done it all with Dom's support and love.

Dom had added his own stipulation before they'd left that hotel room in Dayton: that she move in with him as soon as they returned. That had been a no-brainer for her. She wanted to be near him, sleep with him, make love to him, and wake up to him every morning knowing she was the most loved woman on this planet.

A buzz echoed from the vicinity of Dom's pocket.

Cursing, he removed his cell and glanced at the screen. A second later, he replaced it.

"Who was that?" she asked, backpedaling up the stairs, finding it hard to concentrate on speaking when that hard, tight chest was on full display.

"Ronin," he said, climbing up after her. "Wanted to know if we had any plans tonight."

"Huh. I thought he would've been hunting down the friend Renee brought to Doyle's Friday night. He seemed into her." She frowned. That was an understatement. She'd never seen Ronin as captivated by a woman as he had been at the dive bar. "What was her name? Kim?"

"Uh-huh," Dom murmured. With one swift movement, he shoved down his joggers and kicked the pants down the stairs. *Good God.* His cock rose, flushed, thick, long, and gorgeous. That pulse in her sex ramped up to a full-out rumba. Her nipples peaked, her whole body transforming into a divining rod attuned only for him. "Tenny?"

"Yeah," she breathed, still staring and growing hotter by the second.

"Are you going to talk about Ronin and his love life all night, or are you going to do something with *this*." He swept a hand down his chest and fisted his cock, stroking up, up, up until his hand swallowed the glistening tip. He groaned, and it was one of the sexiest sounds she'd ever had the pleasure of hearing.

"I'll take B, Regis. And that's my final answer." With a snicker, she turned and raced up the rest of the stairs, whipping the jersey over her head.

He was hot on her heels, and she wouldn't have it any other way.

Acknowledgments

Thank you to my heavenly Father, who has made all of this possible. I willingly put all of my hopes and dreams in Your hands, because there's no safer place. Your love for me continues to amaze me.

To Gary, my real-life hero. Now, you might not have long, Jason Momoa–esque locks, but you are my heart and my rock. Thank you for your unfailing love and support. And we can always fix that hair thing. Wig stores, man.

To Dahlia Rose. Our writing challenges got this book done! Well, the writing challenges and the *Lord of the Rings* references and GIFs. LOL!

To Debra Glass. Thank you for your critical eye and bawdy sense of humor. :) Both make you the best critique partner!

To my Football Council. Gary, Daddy, Konard, and Kevin. You guys might tease me mercilessly about my football ignorance, but okay, I kinda deserve it. Hah! But you always come through with the answers, knowledge, and football dialogue. Including the F-bombs. Hee-hee!

To Andie Rutledge. You just brought Seattle alive for me and enabled me to pour that love of your city into this series. Thank you for always being patient and willing to answer any of my questions! You're my Seattle guru, and when I pop up on your doorstep, don't kick me out!

To Rachel Brooks. Thank you for being that rational, put-the-pizza-back-in-the-oven voice. LOL! Your support and experience has been invaluable. And let's just say it. Best. Agent. Evah.

To Tracy Montoya. If the Justice League superheroes were editors, you would be Wonder Woman. And your Lasso of Truth would be your mighty pen. Yep, you're definitely a superhero. And you save my books like they were clueless civilians about to be crushed by a falling building but are too busy gaping to move out of the way. Thank you for ALWAYS swooping in to save the day. AKA, book. AKA, my ass. *whispers* Can I say that?

About the Author

Naima Simone's love of romance was first stirred by Johanna Lindsey, Sandra Brown, and Linda Howard many years ago. Well, not that many. She is only eighteen…ish. Though her first attempt at a romance novel starring Ralph Tresvant from New Edition never saw the light of day, her love of romance, reading, and writing has endured. Published since 2009, she spends her days—and nights—creating stories of unique men and women who experience the first bites of desire, the dizzying heights of passion, and the tender, healing heat of love.

She is wife to Superman, or his non-Kryptonian, less bulletproof equivalent, and mother to the most awesome kids ever. They all live in perfect, sometimes domestically challenged bliss in the southern United States.

Come visit Naima at www.naimasimone.com.

Discover the WAGS series

SCORING WITH THE WRONG TWIN

Also by Naima Simone…

ONLY FOR A NIGHT

ONLY FOR YOUR TOUCH

ONLY FOR YOU

BEAUTY AND THE BACHELOR

THE MILLIONAIRE MAKEOVER

THE BACHELOR'S PROMISE

A MILLIONAIRE AT MIDNIGHT

WITNESS TO PASSION

KILLER CURVES

SECRETS AND SINS: GABRIEL

SECRETS AND SINS: MALACHIM

SECRETS AND SINS: RAPHAEL

SECRETS AND SINS: CHAYOT

If you love sexy romance, one-click these steamy Brazen releases...

PLAYING HOUSE
a *Sydney Smoke Rugby* novel by Amy Andrews

Eleanor is content with her boring life—mostly. She's even fine being the quirky sister in a bevy of beauties. So imagine her surprise when one of her brother's Sydney Smoke mates hits on her at an engagement party. Bodie is shocked the next morning to find the soft, sexy virgin who seduced him with corsets is his best friend's little sister. If he could kick his own ass, he would. Two months later, he's in for an even bigger surprise...

THE BAD GIRL AND THE BABY
a *Cutting Loose* novel by Nina Croft

When Captain Matt Peterson finds himself the guardian of his baby niece, he knows he's in over his head. Then he meets the child's aunt—tough, sexy MMA fighter Darcy Butler—and he knows he's really in trouble!

Dirty Games
a *Tropical Temptation* novel by Samanthe Beck

Quinn Sheridan suddenly has half the time she anticipated to turn herself into an action hero for the role of her career. Luckily, her agent calls in a secret weapon, but the demanding, drop dead gorgeous hardass fails to understand *she's* the client. She has no problem taking direction, but Luke's definition of cooperation feels more like complete and utter submission. And she's tempted to give it to him....

Tempting the Player
a *Gamble Brothers* novel by J. Lynn

After the paparazzi catches him in a compromising position, baseball bad boy Chad Gamble is issued an ultimatum: fake falling in love with the feisty redhead in the pictures, or kiss his multi-million dollar contract goodbye. Too bad being blackmailed into a relationship with a dominant lover like Chad is the last thing Bridget Rodgers needs.